GLIMMERS OF
SCALES

I0678121

EMMA SAVANT

CONTENTS

ACKNOWLEDGMENTS

Thanks go to my editor, Elayne Morgan. She has a magic touch, and this book is a thousand times better for her sharp eye and perceptive comments.

Appreciation is also due to Marita for providing thoughtful feedback, supporting this book from its inception, and answering all my questions about Christmas pudding.

Endless gratitude to my parents for being nothing like Olivia's.

And, of course, many thanks to my husband for his love, support, and willingness to bring me endless cups of tea.

CHAPTER ONE

"I still can't believe we have homework," Lucas said. He flipped a page in *Understanding Biology, 5th Edition.* "It's barely September."

I propped my feet awkwardly on the edge of my seat and let my knees rest against the edge of the pale wooden dining table.

In front of us, Mom's floral centerpiece silently exuded a charm. The magic was meant to make the kitchen feel more "homey" but just made me want to sneeze. I could see the charm's goldenrod-yellow tendrils creeping around us past the edges of my glasses.

I shrugged. "Mr. Hartford likes to get a running start," I said. "This first week's not too bad, though. Why'd you want to do AP Biology anyway?"

"My mom likes to garden," he said. "I figured I could help her more if I knew what was going on."

I took a second to arrange my face like that wasn't the cutest thing I'd ever heard. Mom's bird-themed kitchen clock chirped one o'clock.

"You realize biology and gardening aren't the same thing, right?" I said.

"Now I do," he said. He gave the textbook a sideways look.

Part of me couldn't believe I was so into a guy who didn't even know the difference between biology and gardening. The other part of me—the bigger part of me—was thrilled, because it meant he'd practically *had* to ask for my help, which had meant I'd practically *had* to invite him over.

"You want a drink?" I said.

"Yes," he said.

He sounded desperate for anything that wasn't homework, and I couldn't blame him. His memory for biology was like my memory for Elvish. Dad had forced Daniel and me through three years of lessons and all I could remember was *Where is the bathroom* and *This is the dog of my neighbor.*

"What do you have?" he said.

"Pretty much anything."

"Grape soda," he said. He smirked, like he expected that to be a challenge.

But if I couldn't use my itty-bitty faerie skills in moments like this, what was the point of being a Glim at all?

2

I hid behind the fridge door. A single tap of my finger on a can of ginger ale was all it took. Purple slid across the metal as though the can were being painted by an invisible brush. I held it up in triumph.

"You were saying?"

He grinned and took the can from me. His smile made butterflies do synchronized routines in my stomach. I silently reminded the butterflies for the thousandth time that Lucas had a girlfriend. We were just friends.

The butterflies didn't believe that any more than I did.

I sat back down and pretended to skim the first chapter of his textbook. Not that I needed to skim anything. I knew this stuff like it was my own name. But the book gave me something to focus on, and that was good, because if I looked at him for one more second I was going to turn as pink as the horrible new curtains my mom had just put up in the kitchen windows.

It was impossible to tell what was up with those curtains. My mom had been acting weird lately, and kitchen décor was the least of it.

"So we went over vocab," I said.

I wanted to go over it again, since I was pretty sure he only remembered half the words, but I wasn't going to push it. If he needed more help, he'd just have to come over again.

"What's the assignment?" I said.

Lucas handed me a paper with diagrams of cells on it. I remembered the assignment from when I'd taken the class last year.

I fiddled with the silver ring on my necklace while I watched him fill out the charts and answer questions. I occasionally offered hints like "The word that starts with *organ* and rhymes with *gazelles!*" when he seemed stuck. But after a while, he got the hang of it, and I let my mind wander.

My brain was a carousel these days. The same handful of thoughts rotated by like painted horses: daydreams about escaping to attend a Humdrum university, the silences that had replaced my parents' arguments, my recently less crappy but more stressful job at Wishes Fulfilled, Lucas and his cute smile, Lucas and his horrible girlfriend, and, of course, my personal friend the Faerie Queen. And as soon as I got overwhelmed thinking about that, my brain circled back to college and escape.

The monotony of the thoughts should have bored me, but every subject filled me with either such excitement or dread— or both—that I couldn't do anything but obsess.

"What the heck's a vacuole?" Lucas said.

I jumped. "Storage bubble," I said, too quickly. "They store nutrients and stuff."

"You sound like I just caught you napping in class," Lucas said. "Sorry, this is probably really boring for you."

I shook my head, again too quickly. "No, not at all," I said. "I just have a lot on my mind."

"Anything you want to talk about?" he said.

The list of things I wanted to talk to Lucas about was endless. The list of things I *could* talk to Lucas about without getting arrested for exposing the Glimmering world, on the other hand, was pretty short. He looked disappointed when I shook my head.

"None of it's interesting," I said.

"I doubt that," he said, and it was everything I could do to not lean forward and try to kiss him.

This was getting out of hand. I reached across the table and tapped his homework.

"You," I said. "Focus."

He ducked his head back down, but I caught him glancing up at me like he wanted to say more.

There was no way this was going to end well. I'd never been attracted to someone like this. Imogen was usually the one falling in love with guys—and then dumping them two weeks later. I was usually the one rolling my eyes and saying that, while guys could certainly be nice to look at, there was no point in paying attention to them until college at least.

Lucas made me rethink everything.

And that was not okay, because Lucas was off limits. I was not the kind of girl who went after guys who had girlfriends.

Especially not when those girlfriends looked like supermodels and had more self-confidence in their manicured fingernails than I had in my entire body.

And that should have been the end of the story, but I still couldn't stop stealing looks at him and the way his floppy dark hair fell down over his forehead. He pursed his eyebrows and lips whenever he focused on something, and he kept mouthing the words in the textbook like he was trying to read and memorize them at the same time.

A light knock from the front of the house disturbed our quiet concentration. The front door opened a second later, then slammed.

My best friend, Imogen, walked into the kitchen with her purse over her shoulder and a look of thunder on her face. I glanced over my glasses. The normally golden aura of faerie magic that surrounded her was darker than usual and fizzed with white sparks like glittery bits of lightning.

"What's the matter?" I said.

"We need to talk," Imogen said. "About weddings. And how much they suck."

She slammed her purse down on the table. It created a tiny gust of wind that sent one of Lucas' papers flying to the floor. She did a double-take.

"Oh," she said, deflating slightly. "Hey."

"Hi," he said.

His expression said he wasn't sure whether she was a teenage girl or a feral cat, but he kept his voice neutral. I had the feeling a lifetime of dealing with his dramatic mom had taught him how to disappear.

"Sorry," Imogen said. "I came to get Olivia so we could ride the bus together but I came like twenty minutes early because I swear to all that is holy, if I have to listen to one more band so I can give Maia my opinion, which she will ignore, I will end her."

We'd worn these conversations to death. Imogen's sister Maia was getting married soon, and Imogen had been burnt out on her various sisters' various romances at least two weddings ago. But I was Imogen's best friend, and best friends listened even when they could practically recite the conversation by heart.

She sat down and started massaging her head, dragging her pink nails through her champagne blond hair. "They're releasing a flock of parrots at the end of the ceremony. A flock. Of parrots. Who does that? Doves would be bad enough."

Lucas looked up at me for a second, and it was clear he was thinking the same thing I was: A flock of parrots actually sounded kind of awesome. But neither of us was dumb enough to say that out loud.

Imogen grabbed my soda and took a long sip, then made a face. Imogen didn't like Humdrum drinks. In her opinion, any beverage without fairy dust or eye of newt in it was a beverage wasted.

She let out a long groan and shook her head.

"Anyway," she said forcefully. "I have to get to work."

"You're twenty minutes early," I said.

"Yeah," she said. "And I need ice cream, so we're doing that before we catch the bus. Get your stuff."

I looked to Lucas, but he smiled and said, "Priorities, you know." He began gathering up his papers.

"Give me two minutes," I said.

I went upstairs to my room to grab the blue file folder that held my new case. I tapped it with my wand—which was, as usual, masquerading as a silver hair stick holding my messy bun together—and it shrank until it was small enough to fit neatly into my purse.

A flutter of nerves went through me every time I looked at the folder. It was an interesting case, but not an easy one. For one thing, handling it wrong was likely to get me in trouble with a certain Neptune Pacifica. Nothing like pissing off the king of the Pacific Ocean to start autumn off right.

It probably wasn't healthy to go in assuming I was going to fail, but what else was I supposed to think? I'd destroyed my last case, but through some fluke, the Oracle—the final judge who said whether Stories had been properly fulfilled in a way that brought balance to our world—had thought my screw-ups were all part of some clever plan. I'd gotten lucky. That wouldn't happen twice.

I stopped in the bathroom to see if there was any chance of making my hair look presentable.

There was not.

But while I attempted to enchant the tangles into smooth curls with my wand, my phone buzzed. I checked the message, assuming it was Imogen telling me to hurry up.

This text, though, was from someone else. No number was attached, and where the sender's picture should have been, a seven-pointed gold star flashed and sparkled in a way that was much too alive for a phone screen. The name made my heart trip over a beat.

Amani: Another attack, this one in the Belmont District. Food cart caught on fire. Hum story is hot oil, Glim story is poltergeist, but no traces of poltergeist residue in the area. Just fyi.

My stomach turned over. I'd been getting these texts for months.

Back in the spring, Amani Zarina, the Faerie Queen and the leader of the magical world, had shaken up my life by telling me she wanted to name me as her heir. I'd refused the offer, of course, but I'd accepted a different one. At the beginning of summer, I'd met her underneath a bridge downtown, and she'd asked me to be her eyes.

"My magic is good, but it doesn't catch everything," she'd said.

Her jeans and a plaid button-up had made her look like she was just a normal person out doing her errands. Seeing her standing under a concrete bridge with a big brown purse slung over her shoulder was weirder than seeing a teacher outside of school.

She had tersely explained something I'd already pieced together: Someone, somewhere, was attacking Humdrums all through Portland, and the attacks had been getting worse.

"I don't know why," Queen Amani had said. "I think I know who, but I can't accuse them until I know for sure. A false accusation could ruin so much."

Nothing about it made sense. There was no reason for the queen of all the Glimmering realms to come to me, of all people, about whatever was going on. Maybe she held out hope that I'd eventually agree to become the next Faerie Queen and she wanted to keep me close. Maybe she figured I was the worst Glim she'd ever seen, and that if I noticed something weird going on, it had to be serious.

Whatever the reason, she'd stared at me with her intense gold-green eyes and asked for my help.

I hadn't even wanted to say no.

"This enemy disguises their magic to fit human paranoias and superstitions," Amani had said. A creepy old building would become the site of a "haunting," or an urban legend about snakes in the sewers would spring to life on some poor Humdrum walking alone at night. The goal was fear. No one had died; only a few people had been hurt. But people were getting scared, here and there.

"It's not enough to cause mass hysteria," Amani had said. "If this is who I think it is, panic won't be their goal. They just want to create a little fear here and there, just enough to make people think twice about staying in the city."

She'd switched her purse to her opposite shoulder and glanced cautiously around. I'd glanced around, too. Cars whizzed by over our heads, but down here, in the cool shadow of the bridge, we were alone.

"If we're not careful, they're going to reveal our world to the Humdrums," she said. "Or worse, they'll scare them all out of town."

"Total disaster," I'd said.

There was no way a bunch of emotional faeries and absent-minded wizards were going to keep the garbage collected and the electricity running, no matter how many charms we used to try to automate things. We'd come to depend on Humdrum conveniences, but that didn't mean we knew how to take charge of them.

More compellingly, I'd thought, a world with only Glim-mers would mean my dad would become even more powerful than he already was, and no one needed to deal with that particular headache.

"If you see anything, text me," Amani had said. "You'll find my name already in your phone. The messages will be glamoured—no one can see them but you. But if you run into an emergency, put this on and say my name."

She'd pressed a ring into my hand. It was simple, a silver band set with a tiny mirror surrounded by delicate silver vines.

"It's a direct line to me," she'd said.

Now, it lurked on a chain hidden beneath my shirt. The honor of having a direct line to the Faerie Queen wasn't lost on me, but I didn't want to set it off on accident.

I tapped out a reply to her text.

Olivia: Thanks. Will let you know if I hear anything about it.

I pressed Send, and my stomach flipped over again.

Portland having a secret enemy made me nervous. The part that made me actually queasy was the fact that I hadn't told Imogen.

When Amani had first invited me to visit the Waterfall Palace, I'd lied and told Imogen the queen was only interested in me because I was the youngest godmother Wishes Fulfilled had hired in decades. I hadn't told her about the part where Queen Amani had asked me to be her heir, because I couldn't stand the thought of her freaking out or telling me I'd been wrong to say no.

I hadn't told her when Amani had asked for my help, either. Amani had asked for my discretion. And I really didn't want to talk about the Faerie Queen every time Imogen and I were together, which would have been the inevitable result. And I didn't want our connection to leak to Lorinda, my boss, or— Titania forbid—my parents.

Anyway, how would I even begin that conversation now? It had been months. Imogen would never forgive me for keeping this to myself for so long. Maybe I could just keep it to myself forever, and then someday I'd die and be able to stop worrying.

Thinking sucked. I gave up on my hair, shoved my wand back into it, and raced down the stairs and away from my thoughts.

Imogen and Lucas were in lively conversation. She was complaining about being a bridesmaid, and he was being an awesome listener. I flashed him a quick thumbs-up. Imogen caught the gesture and rolled her eyes at me.

"Come on, weirdo," she said, standing up and winking at me. "Ice cream. Now."

I had to find a way to tell her.

CHAPTER TWO

Our immediate neighborhood was all Victorian mansions and overgrown gardens clambering up and down a forested hillside. As we walked down the hill, the houses got closer together and apartment buildings started showing up. Just beyond that came the best Glimmering ice cream in Portland.

"There were a couple of questions I didn't expect," Imogen said. She pulled the hot pink shop door open for me, and the bell overhead jingled. "Like, there was one about what you should do if you're glamoured as a bird with a broken wing and a princess decides to put you out of your misery instead of bandage you up."

"Does that happen a lot?"

"Didn't used to," Imogen said. "But princesses are feistier than they used to be. I guessed that you should probably hop the hell out of there before she smashes you with a rock. And that was the right answer. I guess a bunch of people said you should drop the glamour and reveal yourself early, but that doesn't even make sense. Revealing yourself as a faerie if you're not either at a crossroads or at the end of the princess' Story is an idiot decision. Talk about wasting your best move."

She examined the brightly colored tubs of ice cream behind the glass counter as she spoke. The shop was tucked between a Chinese restaurant and a stationary store. Any Humdrum could see the door, but it would never cross their mind to walk through it. Imogen tapped on the glass with one long pink nail.

"Kunlun peach, please," she said. "One scoop, waffle cone."

The rosy-cheeked elf behind the counter hopped onto a stool and practically dove into the cooler. She mounded the peach ice cream onto a cone.

"You would be my favorite forever if you put a sprinkle of fairy dust on there," Imogen said.

The woman dipped a spoon into a jar of sparkling purple powder and flicked the glitter onto the ice cream, sending stray bits everywhere.

"Chocolate chunk, please," I said. "Waffle cone. No fairy dust."

And that order just about summed up boring old me.

"I'm glad you have common sense around feisty princesses," I said, while I watched the woman scoop up the chocolate-speckled vanilla.

I'd have picked the same answer, but it would have only been a lucky guess. Unlike Imogen, I wasn't a Glimmering genius who'd just earned top marks on my Proctor Proficiency Exam.

I took the cone from the elf and thanked her. Imogen handed her a couple of small coins and waved goodbye.

"How does it feel to be a licensed Proctor?" I said as I followed Imogen to the door.

"Licensed Junior Proctor," she said. "I need my degree to advance."

"Licensed Junior Proctor, then," I said, and she couldn't stop a goofy smile from spreading across her perfect face.

Being official meant she was free to glamour herself as much as she wanted in front of anyone she liked in order to determine their true character. While normally this idea would have made me nervous, Imogen was good at her job. Better than good. And that mattered, because it was important work. Not many Stories concluded without the moment of truth and nuggets of wisdom Proctors provided as they tested Heroes' and Heroines' moral character.

But being a Proctor was hard, the kind of job that made my work at Wishes Fulfilled look like a vacation. Being a faerie godmother just required that I grant wishes, not make value judgments as to whether my clients deserved them.

Theoretically, anyway. I'd made a million value judgments on Elle's case. But then, I aspired to be a biologist, not a career godmother.

Imogen nudged the door open with her hip and we stepped out into the warm sunlight. I kept pace with her as she strode down the sidewalk.

"Only a Junior for another few years," she said. "Liv, you should come to Institut Glänzen with me. Seriously. We could be roommates. It would be amazing."

A familiar guilt made my stomach twinge, but only for an instant. We'd had this conversation before, but I couldn't change my mind about this any more than I could suddenly up and accept Queen Amani's job offer.

"Glänzen is the most prestigious faerie academy in the world, remember?" I said. "Which means I probably can't get in. Also, I can't go to Oregon State's biology program if I'm in the Swiss Alps."

"You wouldn't be going to some Humdrum biology program, dork," Imogen said. "You'd be, I don't know, doing something awesome."

"Biology *is* awesome," I said. "Glänzen is good if you want to make faerie-craft your life's work."

That wasn't my plan. We'd both known that for a long time.

All my energy was geared toward the future, waiting breathlessly for the moment I'd step onto a college campus and start a new life, studying biology or forestry or whatever plant-related thing ended up making my heart pound the hardest. For the first time, I wouldn't be Olivia Feye: godmother; or Olivia Feye: Reginald Feye's daughter; or Olivia Feye: secret eyes of the Faerie Queen. I would just be me.

And if I was honest, other than knowing that digging my hands into freshly-tilled soil made me want to do a happy dance, I didn't even know what "me" meant. There were so many things I hadn't tried, and so many versions of myself I hadn't become. Life as the daughter of a Glimmering politician was simple: Be good, show up to events, and don't cause trouble. I'd done everything right, except for the time I'd almost ruined Elle's case. But my last year of high school was just beginning, and after I survived that, the whole world would open up.

"You should think about it," she said. "You remember the year I was in France? This is like that, but it's four years instead of one."

"I love you times a million, but I can't give up my life's ambition to be your roommate."

Something flickered across her face, but she rolled her eyes before I could catch the expression.

"Besides, you won't be gone the whole time," I said. "There's summer vacation and Christmas. And it's not like you won't have a magic mirror at Glänzen. We can literally mirror each other every day."

"Mirrors and phones aren't the same," she said. We stepped off the sidewalk to let a woman walking three pugs pass. "Also, don't even try to tell me you couldn't get in. You're the youngest Wishes Fulfilled godparent in, I don't know, maybe ever. I'm still never going to forgive you for that."

"Lorinda said there was one girl back when Wishes Fulfilled started," I said. "But she was the owner's daughter, so I don't know if that counts."

Lorinda, my boss, knew everything there was to know about faerie godparenting. It was usually more than I wanted to hear. She was convinced I was a rising star set to take over the agency. I didn't have the heart to tell her I was only there for the gold.

"Anyway, what would I do there?" I said. "Practice love spells?"

"What are you going to do at your Humdrum college?" Imogen said. "Math homework and essays on plant structure? That's so boring I almost fell asleep in the middle of the sentence."

"Boring for you, maybe," I said.

To me, it sounded like exactly what I'd been looking for all my life. OSU wasn't quite far enough from home, but the in-state tuition meant my biggest dream—the chance to be a normal nobody for once in my life—was almost in my grasp. I wouldn't trade that for the best faerie godparenting education the world had to offer.

Imogen poked my shoulder. "You just want to stay here with Lucas," she said. She winked at me and turned to cross the street. The orange STOP hand was glaring at us, but she twirled her finger and it switched instantly to the white WALK figure. A car screeched to a halt to avoid running the red light that had suddenly appeared in front of it.

I jogged to catch up as she strode across the street. "If I'm not willing to take off to the Alps with you, I'm definitely not going to stay in Oregon for Lucas."

Especially since Lucas had a girlfriend, which Imogen didn't seem to think was as big a deal as I did.

"You could get away from your parents," she said in a sing-song voice.

She was basically holding out candy to tempt me. It was the closest she'd come so far to winning me over, and even though I knew she was teasing, I didn't want to laugh.

Two college-aged guys with giant beards passed us. One of them looked longer at Imogen than was strictly necessary. She didn't even notice.

"No dice," I said. "If I go to Institut Glänzen, I get to be away from my parents for most of the year. If I go to OSU, they'll disown me."

"If only you could be so lucky."

A vague voice in the back of my head said I should feel guilty for talking about my family that way. We never talked like that about Imogen's family.

But then, Imogen's family hadn't earned our dismissal. Her sisters drove her up the wall, but at least they secretly liked each other, and her parents were freaking adorable. My parents hadn't spoken to each other in three weeks, and neither of them were even bothering to act like that was weird anymore.

Maybe that was how I'd managed to keep from telling Imogen about Queen Amani. I came from a whole family of people who never talked to each other about anything. Was it any surprise I had followed so perfectly in their footsteps?

I opened my mouth. She had to know.

"Honestly?" Imogen said before I got a word out. "I hate that you're not coming to Glänzen with me. But I'm glad you're getting to finally do your boring Humdrum thing."

"Me too," I said. "About that."

"If this stupid wedding has taught me anything, it's that I love what a weird Humdrum-lover you are," she interrupted. "I've been surrounded by Maia and her friends the past couple weeks and, like—her friends are exhausting. They're all in school or working these fancy Glim jobs, and every conversation is like they're just trying to out-Glim each other."

I ducked behind her to avoid being run over by an enormous baby stroller.

"How do you out-Glim someone?" I said.

"Like, I'm a Junior Proctor, right?"

"Right."

"So Maia mentions that, and then one of her friends goes, 'Oh, isn't that sweet. I thought about doing that before I decided to work for the Oracle's political advisory council.'" Her voice took on a simpering quality. "And then this other friend starts going off on her schooling to become a Glim doctor, and then another one started blabbing about how *special* she felt as a magical researcher at the university."

"Maia's friends sound obnoxious," I said.

"No freaking kidding," she said. "But it made me appreciate you more. You're never going to try to compete with me for fanciest Glim job. You've never cared about that, and I think that's why we hit it off so well when we were kids. Like, I'm the Glim; you're the Hum. We never have to compete, you know?"

My heart sank.

"That's true," I said.

The bus hissed and clanged to a stop just as we reached the little bus shelter. I crammed the last tiny funnel-shaped bite of my ice cream cone into my mouth and stepped on board.

For maybe the first time, stepping onto the bus to go to work felt like something I wanted to do. Work meant I could push this conversation to the back of my mind. When I was poring through a case file, I didn't have to think about this stupid, heavy secret. I didn't have to think about my parents, either, or my total inability to fall for someone available.

All I had to do was solve one problem, and then another, until I got my client to a happily-ever-after.

And today was better than most, because today I had a new case, and I was going to look over it while enjoying the best shortcake cappuccino in town.

CHAPTER THREE

Every time I stopped by Elle's café, Pumpkin Spice, the wooden vines carved in relief on the backs of the chairs had changed a little. Today, delicately carved blossoms had sprouted on some of the vines. The blossoms seemed to sway gently, though it could have been a trick of the light. Elle said I could expect to see full-grown miniature pumpkins soon, which she hoped to pry off, enchant, and sell at the Portland Saturday Market as charms.

The butterscotch walls seemed warmer, too, lit by new filigree-shaded lamps jutting out of the walls between tables. The brown couches along the right side of the room had been replaced with burnt orange floor cushions surrounding low tables. The room still smelled like a spice cupboard, but there was an extra something here, too—the faint almost-scent of a well-cast enchantment.

I glanced over the tops of my glasses. They shielded me from seeing magic everywhere, which was a rare and somewhat inconvenient faerie gift.

Above the lenses, the room shifted to life, with warm gold sparkles floating down from the filigree lamps and soft orange curls rising from mugs with the steam. The living wooden leaves on the backs of the chairs rustled in a nonexistent breeze.

But the people stood out more than the charms: Everyone here was a Glimmer. Glittering nebulas surrounded the faeries. At a table set into the front bay windows, a cluster of wizards chatted as constellations slowly spun around their heads. A witch's dragon familiar, translucent and emerald green, curled up around her neck and nuzzled her ear beneath her shocking blue hair. The witch was talking to a water sprite who sat in a mist that gave off a faint rainbow if I tilted my head just right. Around the door, a pulsing gold light kept the Humdrums out and drew the Glimmers in.

Pumpkin Spice catered to the magical crowd these days, one hundred percent.

It was a brilliant business move.

Elle waved at me from her spot behind the counter. Her skin glowed, even when I looked through my glasses. The success of her café had her flushed with radiance.

"Caramel macchiato," she said as soon as I reached the counter. Instantly, I realized that sounded ten times better than the shortbread cappuccino I'd been planning on ordering.

Elle had developed an uncanny ability to figure out exactly what people were craving—sometimes better than they could. It was just one of her many blossoming gifts. Her dad was a Humdrum, but her mom had been an earth witch. Elle had inherited a whole slew of abilities, including a certain savvy about anything—including coffee beans—that had started in the ground.

She handed me an orange ceramic mug. The Pumpkin Spice logo was emblazoned on the front, and the pumpkin vines entwined around the name shifted in the light.

"No charge," she said brightly.

She'd forgiven me completely for meddling in her life all spring; I had a feeling Kyle, her best-friend-turned-boyfriend, had something to do with that. He was behind the counter, too, shaking his hips to the pulsing beat of a faerie alt band coming from the radio while he replaced flavored syrups on a wooden rack. I dropped a couple of coins into the tip jar and took my coffee to a table.

I set the small blue folder down. My magic wand was wedged in my hair, holding the curls back in a twist. I touched the wand's handle and the folder sprang back to its full size with a papery rustle.

Client: Lily Pacifica, Princess of the North Pacific Ocean, Twelfth Daughter of King Neptune Pacifica

Age: 19

Occupation: Princess

Hiring Client: Lily Pacifica

Case Summary: Lily Pacifica has fallen in love with a human male, a Humdrum named Evan Costner (see enclosed personal details). She wishes to become human to enable their relationship to deepen. She is the twelfth daughter of the King Neptune Pacifica, king of the North Pacific Ocean, and his consort wife, Queen Muriel.

I wished mer-kings would stop calling themselves Neptune. The king of the North Pacific was named King Neptune. So were the kings of the South Atlantic and the Mediterranean, and so were most of their oldest sons. The king of the North Atlantic was named Bob. I wanted to send him a thank-you note.

Lily's father has contacted Wishes Fulfilled to oversee the case. King Neptune is opposed to inter-species transformations and has hopes of Lily marrying an influential merman within the kingdom and/or pursuing a career relevant to her primary interest area of art/sculpture. King Neptune and Queen Muriel are aware of Lily's decision to contract a Wishes Fulfilled godparent, but have expressed strong hopes that the assigned Godmother (i.e., Junior Godmother Olivia Feye) will be able to redirect Lily's wish to a more productive venue.

Objective: Grant Lily Pacifica's wish, or a wish of equal or greater subjective value.

Recommendations: Redirect Princess Pacifica's aspirations toward a wish more in harmony with her probable future happiness. All parties are aware a Little Mermaid Archetype is likely present; the king and queen prefer to avoid the risks inherent in such an Archetype. Godmother is expressly prohibited from pursuing a Suicide Resolution, as per Oracle's Agreement, Section 3, Clause 3.8.

Relevant Archetype (subject to change at Godparent's discretion): Little Mermaid

I could see why Lorinda had assigned this case to me. My track record for coloring inside the lines wasn't exactly stellar. If anyone could ruin a love affair so badly that it would change Lily Pacifica's mind about this human, it was me.

The photo of Lily had been taken at night. Her skin glowed gunmetal blue in the moonlight. I could make out the banks of the Willamette River behind her. Lorinda had told me that Lily, like many other mermaids living along the coast, often travelled up the river to take in the sights.

"This Evan person is a photographer," Lorinda had said. "He was taking pictures of the skyline and the Willamette. She swam over to say hello, foolish girl, and fell head-over-tail for him."

No one had mentioned whether he'd fallen in love with her, too. If her looks were any indication, it was a definite possibility. Her skin shone like it had been dipped in mother-of-pearl, her red hair cascaded over her bare shoulders like fire in the night, and her eyes had that fierce joy you only ever saw in mermaids, or maybe nyads who didn't leave their rivers much.

As for why Lily thought this relationship was worth leaving her kingdom over, I couldn't say. I couldn't wrap my mind around the idea of leaving the freedom of the water for some guy.

But then, I wasn't a mermaid, and mermaids weren't known for being the most sensible Glims around.

If nothing else, this sea princess seemed to like Humdrums, or at least one of them. Imogen had always accused me of having a "thing" for Humdrums, so maybe that would help Lily and me connect.

I pulled out my phone. A couple of taps brought up the JinxNet in a browser. Glimmering websites weren't exactly on the internet, but the electrical impulses that made the internet possible weren't much different from the energetic impulses that made magic work, and the two systems played so nicely together that some clever magicians had figured out how to lace magic and code together back in the late eighties. It took only a moment of searching to pull up a page on hybrid-to-human transformations.

Less than a minute of reading later, it was clear I had logistics on my side. Turning a half-human into a full human was a headache of a process, and unless we got a transformation specialist or really brilliant witch to cut us a serious deal, it would probably cost more than Lily could pay without her parents' help.

If the other cases I'd heard about were any indication, money was always plenty motivating, even for princesses. Redirecting this mermaid to a different wish should be easy.

My phone vibrated. A text notification rolled up on the top of the screen. I barely registered Lucas' name before my finger swapped the JinxNet out for the message, my hand acting before my mind had time to catch up.

Lucas: So… That went well.

Wondering if I'd missed the first half of our conversation, I replied with a quick *What?* His reply was almost instant, as if he'd typed it before I'd even responded.

Lucas: Aubrey just dumped me.

The pieces refused to connect in my head for a moment, as though the facts had to drag themselves through syrup to meet. When they did—with the words *Lucas, dumped, single,*

Lucas single! sprinting through my mind—my eyes flew wide open.

"Do not overreact," I ordered myself out loud. I forced my finger to take its time across the screen.

Olivia: Are you okay?

I hit Send, and the selfish part of me started mentally doing cartwheels.

Lucas Flynn was single.

It wasn't like he was the only guy on earth I'd ever been interested in. But he was the only guy I'd been interested in lately, and we already had something going for us in the friendship department. His being impossibly attractive was the cherry on top.

But attractiveness had to come second, I reminded myself. Coming first was the fact that he was my friend, and he'd just been dumped, and that sucked.

Probably that sucked. I'd never been dumped. I'd never been in anything serious enough that its end would count as an actual breakup.

My phone buzzed and I jumped, even though I'd been expecting it.

Lucas: I don't know.

My fingers flew over the screen.

Olivia: Do you want to go do something?

Lucas: Not really. I just wanted you to know in case I seem out of it.

I bit the inside of my check. I could be patient.

Olivia: For sure. Take care of yourself, k?

Lucas: I will. Thanks. :)

Olivia: Let me know if I can do anything. :)

He didn't reply. But I couldn't focus on my case for another five minutes, and my heart kept skipping beats the rest of the day.

CHAPTER FOUR

"We can't apprehend terrorists if we don't know who they are," my dad snapped into the phone.

I darted past his office door. Imogen darted after me, and we raced up the stairs together to my room.

She jerked her chin back down the stairs once we were safe on the landing. "Sounds like fun."

I rolled my eyes, though secretly I wished I could linger outside his office door and hear just a bit more of the conversation. I had a feeling he was talking about the same criminal Amani wanted me on the lookout for.

"He's having 'issues' at work," I said instead, like there was nothing to it except his boring job. "Again."

It felt weird, not telling Imogen everything I knew. But trying to explain it all to her felt impossible.

We weren't at a loss for things to talk about, anyway. Lucas was the first thing on both our minds. We sat cross-legged on my bed, Imogen leaning against the headboard, me leaning against one of the bottom bedposts with the wooden pillar digging into my back.

"He texted me too," she said. "About freaking time."

I hadn't realized he had her number, but I was glad. If I was ever going to be with Lucas, he absolutely *had* to get along with Imogen. It was the only non-negotiable criteria for a boyfriend I'd ever settled on.

"I talked to him at school for a minute today and he sounds pretty down," I said. I bit a hangnail on my thumb.

"He probably needs some space," Imogen said. "He's a sweet guy. A breakup's going to be hard on him."

Imogen dated more guys in a year than I had flirted with in my entire life. I'd only ever kissed one person, and that had been a spur-of-the-moment thing with a wizard I barely knew at a summer solstice party over a year ago. It had been a stupid way to waste a first kiss, but then, it wasn't like anyone else was lining up.

Imogen, on the other hand, had experience. She'd gone through two boyfriends this school year, and it was only September. Imogen liked their admiration, but commitment wasn't her thing—she'd once confessed that she liked to dump her boyfriends before they had the chance to dump her. Even so, she knew what she was talking about when it came to relationships. If she said Lucas was still upset, he was.

Imogen nudged me with her foot. "I bet you're happy about it, though," she said.

I flushed.

I didn't usually get flustered over guys. But Lucas had always been different. He'd been one of my best friends at an age when I'd been convinced boys were annoying and dumb, and since he'd come back to town, I'd barely been able to stop thinking about him in the moments I could spare between my Cinderella case, Queen Amani's invitations, and my actual real life full of school and family drama. He made me feel unsettled inside—in the nicest possible way.

It was pointless to deny anything, so I brushed her off with a shrug.

"It's terrible," I said.

"Whatever," Imogen said. "Aubrey was a nightmare. He's hurting now, but he'll get over it when he's with someone who's actually nice to him."

I blushed again.

What was wrong with me? Maybe it was too hot in here. I got up and opened the window to let in some fresh air. The herbs on my windowsill danced in the light breeze.

"You should wait awhile, though," Imogen said as I sat back down. "You don't want to be the rebound girl."

I'd already thought about this. Part of me didn't mind the idea. What could be better than to rush to his side in his hour of need and show him that not all girls were moody and demanding and totally awful?

But Imogen was right. I didn't want his feelings for me to be just misplaced feelings for Aubrey. I knew he liked me for me—why else would he have made an effort to rekindle our friendship when he'd moved back?—but I wanted him to love me for me, too.

The thought made heat creep up my neck.

When I'd settled Elle's case, I'd seen absolute love between her and Kyle. I'd never seen anything like it in real life, but he *loved* her. I knew I was the godmother, not the princess—but was it too much to hope that someone might come to care about me like that, too?

Imogen didn't notice the questions racing through my blood. Having dispensed her advice, she changed the subject.

"I'm applying for next year's Rose Galas," she said. She bit her bottom lip and watched for my reaction.

When she was paying attention, she could feel my emotions almost as quickly as I did, so I didn't bother to hide my surprise.

Every summer, Portland hosted an enormous festival celebrating the City of Roses, complete with a Grand Floral Parade and days of festivities. The week after, the Glimmering world always held its own discreet celebrations: the Rose Galas, a glittering series of parties held in a network of hidden ballrooms and glamoured gardens throughout the city. Out of all the events my parents had dragged Daniel and me to over the years, the Rose Galas were the only ones we looked forward to.

My favorite part was that everyone was invited—not just the Glims, but all their Humdrum relatives, too, and the few Hum politicians and community leaders who knew about us.

And at every party, the Rose Empress held court. She was always a Humdrum. That was a political decision, started by a long-ago Faerie Queen who wanted to strengthen ties between our communities. But the court was open to anyone. Most of Imogen's sisters had been involved at some point or another.

I just hadn't expected Imogen to join them.

"I thought you hated 'superficial pageants,' and Glims trying to out-Glim each other," I said.

"I do," Imogen said. A slight rush of embarrassment rolled off her, though her face was calm. "But, I don't know, it feels like a good way to stay involved with the magical community."

I laughed at the thought of Imogen needing to do some thing to be *more* of a faerie. "Did you ever get un-involved?"

She shrugged. "We'll be graduating school soon, and I thought it might be a good opportunity to do something with the wider Glim world. It's Glims and Hums, so I thought maybe it would be a cool thing for us to do, you know—together."

Her face flushed and she looked down at her hands.

I snorted.

"That's hilarious," I said. "Can you imagine?"

"Right?" she said.

I could picture it now: Me and Imogen, all dolled up and marching in a parade like idiots, with Lucas there as one of the Humdrum guests, cheering us on. The idea made me cringe.

"Obviously you're not going to stay involved in Glim stuff after you graduate," Imogen said. "That would be so dumb."

She laughed, though it sounded a little forced. Too late, I saw how red her face and neck had turned.

"Oh my gosh, I'm so sorry," I said. "Were you serious?"

She waved me off. "No, I was joking. Obviously. The Rose Court is awkward. I'm just doing it for the scholarship. I figure my parents can't tell me what to do at Institut Glänzen if they're not paying for it, right?"

"Solid plan," I said. Her color was quickly returning to normal. I let out a breath I hadn't realized I was holding. "Although, I don't know. Maybe them having a say will be a good thing. I don't know what you're going to do without me there to steer you straight."

As it was, I had a feeling she was going to go through half of Europe's eligible Glim guys within the first week.

A spark of white light shot out of her fingertips, barely visible through my glasses but glowing over the top of them. She twirled the spark absently between her fingers.

"Yeah, because going to different schools means you're *totally* going to stop telling me what to do all the time," she said.

"Right," I said. "Because *I'm* the bossy one in this relationship. That's hilarious."

"My mom's the bossy one. She thinks I should jump tracks and go into private consulting for royalty." She rolled her eyes.

Consulting was a luxurious job if you could get it, but Imogen liked to be involved and on the ground. I couldn't see her pandering to some self-important Glimmering princess who didn't realize aristocratic titles didn't mean what they used to.

A light knock sounded on my door. I called for whoever it was to come in, expecting Daniel. My little brother and I had formed a delicate friendship over the past few months. He occasionally invited me to his theatrical poetry performances, and I covered for him when he needed to sneak out of the house for them.

Instead, my mom stepped in, wearing a tank top and yoga pants, her dark hair pulled back in a just-casual-enough ponytail. In spite of her age and two kids, she looked like a fitness model. Even without help from the faint pink-gold beauty glamour she put on every morning, she was pretty. She had to be—she was Reginald Feye's wife, and the wife of one of the

39

leaders of the Grand Council of Magical Beings had to be on top of her game all the time.

"How are you girls doing?" Mom asked.

"Great, Mrs. Feye," Imogen said brightly.

"We're good," I said, with less enthusiasm.

I didn't know what to make of my mom lately. A few months ago, she'd told me she supported my decision to attend a state college. She hadn't said a word about it since, but I hadn't heard her talking to my dad about his alma mater in Austria lately, either, which I hoped was a good sign. That was where my dad wanted me to go: the Imperial College of Faeries in Austria, to study faerie-craft and prepare for a long, productive career in the Glimmering world.

It wasn't going to happen.

Mom smiled at us, but her mind was somewhere else. The smile looked canned, like it had been sitting on the shelf too long.

"Everything okay?" I said.

"Sure," she said, too quickly. "Things are great. I just wanted to make sure things are going okay for you. Do you need anything? Are you hungry? Bored?"

"Nope," I said. "We're good."

I glanced at Imogen for confirmation. She nodded.

A few seconds passed.

"You sure you're okay?" I said.

The air felt awkward.

Mom shrugged and put a hand on the back of her neck.

"Yeah, of course," she said. "Dad just had to leave for a last-minute meeting so I thought I'd see if you girls needed anything before I head to the gym."

There was more to it than that, but I didn't know how to ask. So I smiled and tried to send a warm gust of appreciation towards her.

"We're great. But thanks."

She waited a second more, then said, "Text if you need me!" and left.

Imogen waited a tactful three seconds after we heard the front door close before she let out a long breath of air.

"So," she said, drawing the word out. "Your mom's not doing great, then?"

I let out a long sigh of my own and leaned back. The wooden bedpost dug in hard against my spine. I wiggled side-to-side until the pole shifted enough that the pain faded to discomfort.

"I have no idea what's going on," I said.

I sucked on the inside of my cheek while Imogen looked at me with expectant eyes. She was familiar and safe, but even so, it was hard to tell her the truth about my family. We'd spent our whole childhoods complaining about our parents and siblings, but this was different.

"My parents aren't doing so hot," I finally said. "They've been fighting a lot lately."

Imogen shifted, tilting her head.

"They always fight."

"This isn't even fighting, really," I said. "They just don't talk. They'll be in the same room together and it's like the other person's not even there."

She tossed the spark up into the air. It disappeared with a twinkle.

"Is that better or worse than them screaming at each other?"

"I have no idea," I said. I lifted my hands in a shrug, then let them drop back into my lap. "I just—I'm worried."

The truth spilled from my lips. I hadn't allowed myself to think those words, let alone say them.

"They're not even sleeping in the same room anymore."

Her mouth rounded into a small O.

"Ouch," she said.

"Mom's been in the guest bedroom for a couple weeks. And they're not talking. Dad got in some trouble at work a while ago, I guess. Someone's been messing with Humdrums all over town and no one's been able to catch them yet. Everyone's looking, but somehow it's his responsibility, and he's super stressed about it."

Though I'd never say it out loud, rescuing him from the pressure of his job was another reason I actually wanted to help Queen Amani.

I didn't normally care about my dad's job, or his stress levels. He'd never cared about mine. But this was different. I'd kept my eyes peeled, not just for the queen, but also because some tiny part of me was crazy enough to believe my vigilance might be the thing that could keep my parents from falling apart.

"He and Mom were fighting a lot, but now it's like they both just shut down," I said. Now that the words were out, I couldn't seem to stop them. "Feel the air. There's nothing there, not even arguments."

Imogen's gaze softened and she tilted her head as though listening. Her empathetic faerie gifts were stronger than mine; I was surprised she hadn't already figured out that all was not well in the Feye house. After a moment, she nodded.

"I can feel it," she said. "I think that's it, anyway. Something feels kind of empty and thick."

"The weight of a thousand stubborn silences," I said. "I don't know how much longer they're going to be together."

With no warning, my throat closed up. I looked at the ceiling, hoping the tears that had just leapt to my eyes would stay there.

I hadn't realized it meant so much to me until now.

I hadn't had a good relationship with either of my parents in years, maybe ever. And they hadn't had a good relationship with each other since my dad had been promoted three years ago.

Somehow, though, it was still important to me that they be together. It was still important that we be a family.

"Hey," Imogen said, kicking my knee softly with her foot.

I swallowed hard and tried to look at her, feeling stupid. A moment later, her arms were around me.

"It's okay," she said, voice gentle. "It's okay to be upset."

"It's stupid," I said, forcing myself to be brisk so the tears would be frightened away. "It's not like I haven't seen it coming."

"Seeing a punch coming doesn't make it hurt less," Imogen said.

A garbled laugh scratched its way up my throat. "You sound like a fortune cookie," I said.

"I am a freaking fortune cookie," she said. "What do you think Proctors do all day?" She sat on the bed next to me, leaning her shoulder against mine. "You don't have to be okay with it."

I wasn't okay. But my parents' marriage was falling apart no matter how I felt about it.

"It'll work out in the end," Imogen said. "Love stories always work out in the end."

We both knew better than that. We were Glimmers. We made fairy tales happen. We didn't live them.

CHAPTER FIVE

Numbers swam before my eyes. If I didn't know better, I'd think someone had glamoured my vision.

"I need a break," I said.

The first twinge of a headache was starting between my eyes.

"No way, Liv," he said. "You can't get a degree in a science if you can't do math. You're only on question nine."

He'd called me Liv. No one but Imogen and Daniel called me Liv. I loved the sound of it coming out of his mouth.

"I hate question nine," I said, but turned my attention back to it anyway.

He sat there patiently while the numbers jumbled in my brain and my mom's bird clock ticked softly in the background. The painted songbirds on its surface usually flew around the clock face. Today, though, they'd been still for the better part of two hours. Like most Glimmering homes, ours had a giant Humdrum safety spell cast over the property. As long as Lucas was here, the clock wouldn't spring to life, the doorbell wouldn't announce the names and intentions of any visitors, and my family would keep their drama to themselves.

Except for the homework part, it was a slice of heaven.

"I thought most science people were also math people," he said.

He stretched his leg out across the creamy living room carpet. There was furniture in here, but the floral couches were stuffy, the kind of furniture meant for looks rather than sitting. I leaned back against one couch and propped my notebook up against my knees.

"That's a stereotype," I said. "Shut up, I'm trying to figure out..."

I fell silent and concentrated. Eventually, I found my way to a number that seemed right. He leaned over to check it, and his breath tickled my ear.

"Good job," he said.

A thrill ran down my spine. It felt delicious.

Even better, though, was that I didn't have to pretend it didn't. I wasn't going to be the rebound girl. But I was beyond ready to daydream.

"So what have you been up to the last few years?" I said.

"Math," he said. He tapped his pencil on my notebook, but I put the book down.

"Seriously," I said. "I need a break. My brain is about to explode."

"Sounds messy," he said.

"The walls would get plastered in numbers," I said. "My mom would never get them all off. You don't want to be responsible for that, do you?"

He laughed. It was the first time he'd laughed since he'd showed up. A little of the solemn, just-got-dumped expression left his face.

I nudged his foot with mine.

"You didn't answer my question," I said. "It's been awesome to see you again, but I've still never really heard what you did in between then and now."

Lucas leaned his head back until it bumped against the stiff arm of the couch. A few strands of dark hair slipped away from his forehead.

"Just this and that," he said. "We moved to Arizona, and then we moved to Colorado for a while, and then we went back to Arizona for Mom's job."

"She's a nurse, right?"

"Yeah," he said. "Pediatric nurse. Works with kids."

"What's Arizona like?" I said.

"Hot," he said. "Except everywhere's air conditioned, so really cold at the same time."

I'd never been to Arizona. Anywhere that dry made me nervous. I'd only been to a desert once, during a trip to visit one of Mom's friends in Nevada when I was a kid. I wasn't much of a faerie even then, but the lack of growing green things had still made me nauseated and weak.

"What did you do in Arizona and Colorado?" I said.

He shrugged.

"Not an answer," I said.

"I don't know, normal stuff," he said. "Went to school, hung out with my friends. I got to see my dad a lot last summer, which was great."

He glanced at me like he wasn't sure if he was allowed to talk about his dad. I widened my eyes and lifted my eyebrows, trying to make my face as encouraging as possible.

I'd met Lucas in middle school, and his parents had been divorced for years by then. I'd never heard him talk about his dad.

"He's a long-haul trucker," he explained. "We text a lot but I don't get to see him very much. He let me ride with him on some short trips."

"That sounds really fun," I said.

"It was cool," he said. "Did you know semi-truck cabs have beds in the back?"

"No kidding?"

"No kidding," he said. "We rented a car in between two of his jobs and went camping in southern Utah. The landscape there is unreal."

He pulled his phone out.

"This isn't going to do it justice at all, but I have some pictures on here. I have better ones on my computer at home. Here."

If these were his just so-so pictures, I couldn't imagine what the real ones looked like. Enormous red cliffs rose up toward a cloudless blue sky. In one picture, a river snaked along the bottom of a canyon whose red walls glowed like fire in the evening light. In another, a crescent moon shone from the middle of a red stone arch.

"These are gorgeous," I said.

I slid my finger across the screen and was startled to see a selfie of Lucas grinning next to a bearded man I assumed was his dad. They had the same sparkling eyes.

Lucas shifted next to me. I reached the last picture in the album, but kept scrolling so that the first one came up again.

"Seriously, I can't believe you took these on a phone," I said.

"I have a lens attachment," he said. "Makes a phone camera a little better than a phone camera."

His energy felt almost embarrassed. I turned to look at him.

"You're a photographer," I said.

"Kind of," he said.

"No, not kind of," I said. "Like, you're seriously a photographer."

The world's most horrible thought crossed my mind.

"You don't happen to take a lot of pictures of the Willamette River, do you?" I said.

"No," he said, confused.

Of course he wasn't Evan Costner. Of course my new client wasn't in love with him. And of course I was already getting jealous of any beautiful girl who might be even vaguely connected with him.

I forced my breathing to slow.

"Just curious," I said. "I've heard it's a good place for pictures."

"Maybe I'll have to check it out," he said.

"Maybe I'll have to come with you," I said. The words left my mouth before I could think. But he smiled, and I didn't take them back.

I didn't want to hand the phone back, but I did.

"Do you want to be a photographer?" I said. "Like, for a job?"

"Maybe," he said. "Actually—" He fidgeted with the hem of his shirt. I picked up my pencil and fiddled with it, forcing

51

myself to wait. "Actually, I'm thinking about doing something with film," he finished.

"Yeah?"

"Yeah, I think it would be cool to major in film in college. Pointless, right?"

"No, it's not," I said. "That's awesome. I didn't know you were into that."

"Aubrey thought it was stupid," he said.

He immediately looked away. I felt a small push of awkwardness come off him. I couldn't tell if he wished he hadn't mentioned her, or if he just wished he hadn't mentioned her in front of me.

Well, at least we could get clear on where I stood.

"Aubrey's an idiot," I said flatly.

A small smile touched the corner of his mouth.

"I figure, I like photography," he said. "And I like stories. Not just stories, but, like, the *structure* of stories. You know what I mean?"

I'd never wanted to tell Lucas about my gifts or my world, even if it had been legal. For a split second, though, I wished I could tell him about Archetypes. He'd get a kick out of it. I bit back a laugh and nodded.

"I think it would be awesome to explore how to tell stories in such a complicated medium," he said. "With film, it's not like you're doing one thing. You get to work with visuals and images, but then you're also working with dialogue, and sound. You're even working with time. How many art forms let you work with time?"

"Music," I said.

"Yeah, music," he said. "But music's in films. Movies are like a buffet where you get to sample everything." His eyes lit up, sparkling like they had in the picture with his dad. "It's so powerful. With a good movie, you directly affect people's emotions. It's almost magic, if you think about it. You can actually put thoughts and emotions into someone else. It's freaking amazing."

Rebounds be damned.

"We should go to a movie together," I said. "You can show me exactly what you're talking about."

The tiny crease at the corner of his eye spread. "I'll make you a deal," he said. He picked up my notebook and handed it to me. "You finish this assignment and I'll take you to whatever you want to see."

"Get me popcorn?" I said.

"Let's find out," he said, and nudged my knee with his.

I practically buried my face in the paper, desperate to hide my smile.

CHAPTER SIX

I eyed the tall stone building next to me. It was old and imposing, with carved cornices and arched windows fitted with glittering glass panes. I looked down at the thick creamy paper in my hand again. The golden star on the invitation flashed and twirled; this was the right place.

It sure didn't look like a "Garden of Glims" to me.

I walked up a flight of stone steps to the enormous wooden door, which was at least twice my height. When I pushed it open, cool air from a shadowed lobby surged out to greet me.

"Welcome," a voice said.

When my eyes adjusted, I made out a slender faerie in a tuxedo. Past the edges of my glasses, the swirling nebula of his magic glimmered in shades of green. His dark hair was neatly slicked back from his face.

I, like an idiot, had come wearing jeans.

"Hi," I said. I took a couple of steps forward. "I'm not sure if I'm in the right place."

I held out the invitation. He took it from me and waved one of his manicured hands over it. A silver sheen glinted across the paper and was gone.

He bowed. "Welcome, Miss Feye. Right this way. Her Majesty is expecting you."

My stomach flipped over.

This was not what I'd expected to do today. Lucas had barely left yesterday before one of Queen Amani's flying paper airplanes had flown into my bedroom window and hit me in the head. The note on it had been simple: Queen Amani wanted to "catch up and discuss my future."

I had a feeling I knew what she wanted to talk about, and I knew I didn't want to talk back. But she was the queen, and I was at least going to do her the courtesy of having this conversation in person.

The doors behind the faerie looked like they should lead into a ballroom or chapel. They were tall, heavy, and carved with vines.

"If you'll follow me," he said, and put a hand on the door.

The vines shifted like snakes.

And then I was blinded by light and greenery. I didn't bother trying to hide my gaping as the faerie led me into one of the most beautiful places I had ever seen.

The entire center of the building was flat-out missing. Judging by the size of this place, so was the center of the building next door.

I'd expected to walk into a hallway or a room. Instead, we stepped under a grape arbor and into an enormous brick-walled garden. Sunlight filtered through leaves and turned the air a dappled green.

I followed the faerie down mossy steps to a path of paving stones. They wound through the enclosed garden and disappeared behind a tightly growing cluster of cherry trees in full, out-of-season bloom.

"Whoa," I said, like a genius.

"Is this your first time visiting the Garden?" the man asked.

"I didn't even know this was here."

"It's quite exclusive," he said. "We often reserve it for Her Majesty's private use."

I touched the soft yellow petals of a flower I didn't recognize. The petals dissolved into a cloud of fingernail-sized butterflies at my touch. They rose into the air and fluttered around my head with a sound like distant, tinkling bells. I cringed and clasped my hands behind my back, but the faerie just smiled.

"Mustard Moths," he said. "Neither mustard nor moth, just an enchantment bred into the genome."

I looked at one of the butterflies, which had landed on a red rose the size of a dinner plate.

"You can do that?"

"Of course," he said. "The natural world is the source of faerie magic. It makes sense that our magic can manipulate it, don't you think?"

I frowned and looked around, wondering how many unfamiliar plants were in this place.

"I hadn't thought of it like that."

He led me around a small koi pond, where dozens of glittering orange and yellow fish glided under their ceiling of water lilies. I almost crashed into him before realizing he'd stopped.

He bowed deeply, and I looked up to see Queen Amani sitting at a wrought-iron table in a little cobblestone-covered clearing.

She was in jeans, too.

I was trying to decide if I should bow when the faerie straightened and waved me toward her with one sweeping, formal gesture.

"Olivia!" Queen Amani said brightly. "I'm so glad you could make it. Thanks, Peter."

The faerie—Peter—bowed again.

He walked away along the winding garden path, and I was left to advance awkwardly toward the table, where Queen Amani's crazy whirling vortex of magic spun around her in a burst of shimmers and gold just beyond the edges of my glasses.

"Have a seat," Amani said.

She nodded toward the chair across from her, and it slid itself neatly out for me. She glanced up to where Peter was just disappearing behind the cherry trees, and then propped her feet on one of the chairs to her side.

"Tea?" she said.

My mouth was dry. "Yes, please," I said.

She leaned back in her seat, tipping the chair onto two legs, and plucked a couple of purple blossoms from the star-shaped flowers growing behind her. She dropped the petals on the table and waved her hand over them.

The silky petals grew and wrapped around each other, growing up into the shape of a purple kettle and two cups on saucers. Golden streaks that used to be the flowers' stamens swirled across the dishes like smeared lines of paint. Despite my nerves, I leaned forward, transfixed.

Queen Amani lifted the kettle lid and snapped her fingers, and a miniature gray cloud, no bigger than my fist, formed above our table. A tiny torrent of sweet-scented rain poured from the cloud into the kettle, accompanied by flashes of lightning and thunder so soft they may as well have been our chair legs scraping on the cobblestones.

When the kettle was full, Amani snapped again. The cloud dissolved and the water churned to a furious boil. Seconds later, she was pouring steaming floral tea into my cup.

"That was awesome," I said.

"Right?" she said. "I had to practice forever but it's a hit at parties."

I sipped at the tea. It was exactly hot enough, and I had a feeling it wasn't going to cool anytime soon. A bright red bird fluttered out of one tree behind the queen and into the branches of another.

"I had no idea this was here," I said.

Amani looked around and sighed, a happy sigh I recognized as the one I gave whenever I was alone in our community garden. The sunlight kissed her dark skin with gold.

"Four-hour meetings discussing trade restrictions on elven jewelry can be a little tedious, but you hold them here and suddenly, bam, you don't mind at all," she said. "It's honestly one of the best perks of being queen."

She lowered her teacup. "Speaking of which."

The sweet, rosy tea settled in my stomach like lead. I set my cup down and waited. This was the reason I was here, and the reason I hadn't entirely wanted to come.

"Have you reconsidered?" she asked.

The right words wouldn't come to my mouth—the eloquent, gracious ones about being so honored she'd considered me to make this valuable contribution to the Glimmering world, but, regretfully, I had to decline.

"No," I said instead. That didn't feel like enough, so I added, "Sorry. I'm happy to keep helping you in other ways, though."

Her frown was barely perceptible. But she swallowed it back and replaced it with a smile.

"That's okay," she said. "I didn't really expect you to have changed your mind."

"Sorry," I said again.

"No, it's fine," she said. "I apologize. I just…"

She blew out a heavy sigh and leaned forward.

"I keep seeing you," she said. "In my divination pool. Every time I try to find my heir, you're still there. And you shouldn't be, because you made a choice *not* to be my heir, and your choice should have affected the future. I was hoping maybe you weren't fully committed."

Maybe saying it aloud in a firm voice would help. "I'm fully committed," I said.

I willed the garden around me to listen. And I willed Queen Amani to listen. Despite the fact that my mom was apparently brilliant at it, I didn't really get how divination worked. Maybe

Amani nurtured subconscious hopes that I'd accept, and that was why she kept seeing me in her pool?

Because the queen of the Glimmering world was totally wasting her valuable time pining about the career choice of the great Olivia Feye. I wished Imogen was there to kick me under the table.

Not that Imogen knew about any of this.

I had to find a way to tell her.

The urge to get up and run consumed me in an instant. I squeezed my toes inside my shoes and forced myself to stay still.

"I don't blame you," Amani said. "I was never going to choose this."

I frowned at her. I wasn't sure if I believed her. She was too in her element here.

"No sane person would. But this work chooses you," she said. A soft smile tugged at her lips. "I don't regret it. It's a hell of an adventure."

"Not my kind of adventure," I said.

But Queen Amani already knew that. She pushed back from the table. "Oh well," she said. "You want to walk around, since you're here?" she said. I shot to my feet.

The garden was even bigger than it had seemed at first glance. I couldn't tell if the glamour draped over the space like a net made the garden seem bigger than it was, or if the glamour was actually on the walls around us, making the buildings seem smaller on the outside than they were in here.

The stately buildings I'd seen when I'd arrived were a complete façade; even the windows, which seemed so convincing from the street, were gone here. Instead, crumbling red brick rose around us on every side, the same kind of brick that seemed to make up half of Portland. Laced over the brick were ivy, roses, faerie lace, clematis, wizard's blood, and other climbing plants I didn't recognize. They stretched above us, creeping higher up the walls than I would have thought possible.

Amani let me walk in silence for a while. I forced myself to breathe, filling my lungs and focusing on the plants and the way my belly rose and fell with each breath.

"Maybe it's not about you," she said at last.

She sounded like my dad might, if he knew about any of this. *Not everything is about you, Olivia,* I could practically hear him saying. *Have you even considered your responsibility to your community? This world has gifted you with privilege, Olivia, and I will not see you waste it.*

"Maybe you're just supposed to give me a clue," Amani said.

She smiled at me, and I remembered exactly how unlike my dad she actually was.

It was weird to consider that maybe all powerful Glims weren't as uptight and demanding as my dad was. From his stories of Council meetings and the kind of people he brought home for schmalzy dinners, I'd assumed that everyone who was anyone in the Glimmering world was pretentious and boring. Amani was neither.

Queen Amani kicked off her shoes and sat cross-legged on the edge of another koi pond. She trailed her fingers in the water and started making kissy faces at the fish.

"Titania, they're cute," she said. "I never would have thought fish could be cute, but look at their little faces."

It was impossible not to laugh. The fish seemed to be trying to kiss her back. They nuzzled at her fingers with their tiny round mouths.

She waved her free hand in lazy circles in the air. A moment later, two balls of watermelon shimmered into being in her palm. She held one out to me. The juice dripped down between my fingers.

"Hold it right at the surface," she instructed.

I did, and the fish swam up to me and devoured the melon, their mouths making sucking noises at the surface of the water. I stared, transfixed, and she handed me another.

She was right. They were adorable. The fish churned the water below me. I could barely make out my reflection in all the ripples.

"I don't know why I'm still showing up in your divinations," I said. "Do I need to, like, write an official letter of refusal or something?"

"Maybe," she said, and laughed.

She pushed her hand up through her dark hair, making the tangle of curls move as one big mass. I caught a glint of a golden earring before her hair fell back to cover it.

"I think it's more that I still have something to learn from you," she said. "You're going to tell me something that helps me figure out who the next queen is going to be."

"Like what?"

She shrugged and tossed a piece of watermelon out into the water. The fish were on it before I had a chance to see whether it would sink or float.

"If you had to pick one thing you wanted in a queen, one thing you would choose to focus on if you were to take the job, what would it be?"

I splashed my fingers in the water. "I don't know."

"Another melon ball says you do," she said, holding one up.

"Fine," I said.

I took the fruit from her and held it out for the fish. I *didn't* know, so I spoke without thinking, hoping my mouth would be smarter than my brain.

"I think… I think the next queen needs to have a strong plan for how we're going to handle the relationship between our community and the Humdrums," I said. "This person who keeps attacking them? I'm not making excuses for them, but maybe their actions are a symptom of a bigger issue? There aren't a lot of guidelines on how to be a Glim in a Humdrum world. Sometimes I feel isolated from the Hum world. Maybe... Maybe other Glims feel stifled."

She tilted her head and stared at me, her greenish eyes wide. They looked too green against the warm brown of her skin, like the dappled sunlight was coming through her.

"You'd rather be a Hum, wouldn't you?"

"Will I get arrested for treason if I say yes?"

"No." She laughed. "Those are good points. You haven't heard more about that person, have you?"

"The one attacking the Hums?"

"Mmhm."

I shook my head. "I would have told you if I did," I said. "I haven't heard anything new."

She sighed. "Well, that's something. I'm calling them Eris, by the way. They're being melodramatic enough that I decided they needed a stupid code name. Eris is the Greek deity of chaos."

Irritation edged her voice like poison on a knife. She took a deep breath and shook her head.

"Okay, what else?" she said, changing tone completely. "If you had to choose two things for the next queen to focus on —"

"You're just going to keep going with this, aren't you?" I said.

She shrugged, and I chewed on the inside of my cheek.

"Okay, another thing that I think the next queen should focus on is…"

I trailed off. My life already felt so suffocated with magic that I'd never tried to figure out what was going on in our wider world. I just wanted to escape it. I wanted this conversation, and the person attacking the Humdrums, and the issue of Amani's heir all to be settled so I could focus on college applications and be done with all these questions.

"I really don't know," I said. "I haven't been paying attention."

"Maybe that's it, then," she said. "Maybe the point is that I'm supposed to find someone who doesn't care what's going on in our world."

That sounded like a recipe for disaster. "No," I said. "What you probably want is someone like my best friend, Imogen. She knows everything that's going on and then some. She'd be a much better queen than I would."

The ever-present guilt at not telling Imogen about any of this flared.

"Imogen," Amani said, like she was tasting the name. "Tell me about her."

I met her gaze. She was twice as interested all of a sudden. Imogen's name had sparked something. Maybe it was hope. Maybe Amani's divination skills had finally picked up on why I was supposed to be in the picture.

I wished the divination could have just made Imogen appear in the first place and left me out of it.

"She works at Wishes Fulfilled with me," I said. "She's my age, but she's a much better faerie. She's a Proctor with Wishes Fulfilled's Department of Tests and Quests and she just aced her Proctor Exam. She's really good at glamours and she's going to Institut Glänzen after she graduates."

I couldn't have invented a better resumé for a possible Faerie Queen. It had taken the words leaving my mouth to realize how obvious it all was. Of course Imogen was meant to for this job.

"She'd be an amazing queen," I said. "She's smart, she's driven, she's obsessed with being a good faerie. And she's got leadership abilities, too. I'd follow her just about anywhere. She's the kind of person who does things with purpose, you know?"

This morning, I had not imagined I would be spending the afternoon in a secret garden trying to convince the Faerie Queen to basically adopt my best friend.

Then again, things usually didn't end up how I imagined them.

Maybe I wouldn't have to tell Imogen about Amani's offer. Maybe she'd get an offer of her own.

"She sounds interesting," Amani said. "Institute Glänzen is a competitive school."

"It's been her plan since we were kids," I said.

"And what about you?" Amani said. "You're planning on studying biology, right?"

"Or horticulture," I said. "Or permaculture, or agriculture, or ecology. I'm not sure yet. It will definitely be at a Humdrum school, though."

"Yes, I remember," she said.

A fish swam up and started suckling on her fingers, which still dangled in the water. She started and pulled her hand away.

She stood up. "Come check out the rest of the garden," she said.

The path seemed to wind back on itself until I was lost. Amani parted the drifting branches of a weeping willow and I stopped to examine some button-like purple flowers that grew near its base. She explained that they were called Knots of Concord and had to be carefully cultivated by skilled faeries, as they were too delicate to survive most environments.

"The shelter of the tree is good for them," she said.

"The enchantment doesn't hurt, either."

"You can feel that?" she said.

"Nope," I said. I pulled down my glasses a little, and the pearly shimmer of magic that surrounded the flowers like mist filled my view. "I'm not great at feeling magic. But I can see it. Hereditary thing. I got it from my grandma."

"That must be useful," Amani said. She leaned against the willow like it was a friend. "The only hereditary magic I got was a knack for creating charms."

"It's kind of annoying, honestly," I said. "I have to wear glasses to block it or it's too distracting."

She held out a hand, and I handed my glasses to her. Instantly, my vision was clouded with the flowers' enchantment and Amani's own sparkling gold vortex of energy. She examined the lenses.

"Elf-made," she said. I nodded.

It was a relief to get them back on my face.

"Tell me more about Imogen," Amani said, turning and walking out of the shelter of the willow canopy.

Without being able to say why, I felt myself flush. I was glad Amani was ahead of me and couldn't see my face, though she could probably feel my emotions just as well as I could.

Not that I could quite pin down what I was feeling.

"We've been friends since we were little," I said. "We both had to go to faerie camp every summer. I hated it, but she loved it. Once I was with her, I started to love it too."

"And you think she'd make a good queen?"

Again, a feeling I didn't quite have a name for stirred in the pit of my stomach. If I were younger and Imogen wasn't my best friend, I might have called it jealousy. But that was impossible. For one thing, it was about being the Faerie Queen. For another, it was *Imogen*.

"I know she would," I said.

"What are her goals?" Amani asked.

We passed a thin waterfall that tumbled from the top of the brick wall and down into a sparkling emerald pool. I stopped and watched the water for a moment, its clear streams turning to white froth as the waterfall ran over irregularities in the brick.

"She's going to become a Proctor after school," I said. "She'll be a good one. I don't know if she's planning on staying with Wishes Fulfilled, but whatever she does, she's going to be great at it."

She was great at everything. She was beautiful, her magic was strong, and she cared about our world in a way I didn't understand.

I kicked a pebble on the path ahead of me, refusing to meet Amani's curious gaze.

"Seriously," I said, trying to calm the unease that clawed at my insides. "She'd make an amazing queen."

CHAPTER SEVEN

I hadn't been sitting at my desk two minutes when a blur of white swooped above me. A soggy scroll dropped on my desk. I looked up to see a seagull fluttering down to land on the edge of my cubicle. It turned its head and stared at me with a wide yellow eye.

I pulled apart the seaweed that held the paper together. Words crawled across the page in glistening green ink:

Dear Faerie Godmother,

I write to inform you that I will need to postpone our meeting. As I believe you have been informed, my father is strongly opposed to my seeking your services, and has engaged me for several royal functions this week for purposes of creating a scheduling conflict. I offer my sincere apologies and assure you this will not happen again.

Please review the enclosed calendar and select the date that would be most convenient for you. You may send the note back with my bird.

I hope this will not delay us too long. I am anxious to begin the next stage of my life!

Regards,

Princess Lily Pacifica, Pearl of the Pacific and Duchess of the Willamette River

I was itching to meet the princess, so I scanned the calendar, marked the earliest day that would work, and tied the note to the bird's leg. With some concentration and a couple of extra jabs of my wand, I managed to turn a pencil into a beetle. The bird plucked the wriggling bug up, nodded to me in thanks, and flew away.

Princess Lily was a hard mermaid to meet. Fortunately, her Humdrum crush, Evan Costner, was much easier to track down.

I couldn't shoo Lily away from Evan without at least knowing something about the guy, so I'd spent most of the morning studying him online until my eyes felt like sandpaper.

Evan was a successful photographer, which meant he had accounts on just about every major social media and photo-sharing site out there. His personal website showed image after image of Portland. Crumbling brick buildings, gray skies heavy with clouds, and the riverfront busy with boats scrolled above a black background. At the top of the page, a minimalist header said *A SENSE OF PLACE* in thin, mint-green letters. From there, a tab labeled *Humanity* led to a few series featuring attractive models.

In the first series, a girl with high cheekbones and long legs posed on park benches and against parking meters, wearing a rainy-day ensemble of matching raincoat, galoshes, and floppy-brimmed hat. The clothes were too curated to belong to a real person. The next set showed a dark-haired girl with windswept hair and a white sundress, slouching around a yacht.

His photos were beautiful—a little too beautiful. The models exuded a self-conscious hippie vibe that felt like advertisement instead of art. Maybe that could count as "superficial and materialistic" when I talked to Lily? I made a mental note.

Information on the man himself, though, was hard to find. My Wishes Fulfilled logins gave me unlimited access to almost every social media page out there. If someone posted something, I could find it, no matter what their privacy settings. But Evan didn't talk much. His posts were all photos, and the photos didn't tell me anything except that he'd had a brief love affair with sepia tones last year, preferred models with big eyes, and had recently become interested in the way the lights of the city played on the river.

Taking river photos was how he'd met Lily, of course. I still wasn't sure how she'd managed to make that seem normal. He was a Humdrum, after all, and a tail seemed like a hard thing to hide.

I was about to leave his professional photography page when a comment on one of his latest pictures caught my eye. The profile picture attached to the comment was of a pretty girl with long dark hair—the same one, I realized, who'd been in the slouchy yacht photos.

Isabelle Sheridan: Gorgeous series, love. So proud & can't wait to be your Mrs. Costner! <3

The comment was dated a week ago.

My eyes widened and I read the comment again.

Mrs. Costner?

Not only was he a Hum and wildly ineligible to be the consort of a sea princess, but he was also engaged.

I wanted to high-five this girl. A fiancée would scare Lily off even better than I could.

I clicked out of the browser, set the computer to hibernate and grabbed my purse off the floor. I liked morning shifts— even when they felt long, like this one had, I was out in time for lunch and had the rest of the day to myself.

It had been a long week, and an afternoon at the community garden where I volunteered was just what I needed to get myself right-side up again. The squash plants were overloaded and I couldn't wait to harvest a whole bag of them, then spend the rest of the afternoon gathering heirloom hollyhock seeds for next year.

Nerd, I could practically hear Imogen say in my head.

She still hadn't texted me back about my date with Lucas. I hoped it was a date, anyway. If nothing else, Imogen would be the person who could pick a movie that would turn it into one. But in between Maia's wedding prep and some advanced Proctor training, she'd somehow managed to wiggle out of school for three days. I didn't expect to get any real conversation from her until things calmed down.

Imogen had a thousand and one talents, but responding to texts when she was busy was not one of them.

I pressed the elevator button and waited, my toes practically dancing in my shoes.

Wishes Fulfilled was hidden on the top floor of a performing arts center downtown. An elevator no Humdrums ever seemed to notice was our only way in and out, and I rode down to the first floor while visions of rich soil, healthy leaves, and popcorn at the movies danced through my head.

The doors slid open to the lobby.

I wasn't surprised to see Imogen standing there. She'd had afternoon shifts lately. But the person with her was the last one I'd expected to see.

Lucas.

A thrill flooded through me. I should have known Imogen would come through and find a way to push us together. She was the best.

I took a deep breath and geared myself up to wave or say hi or otherwise not trip all over myself when he looked over at me.

But he didn't look over.

"Have a good day," Lucas said to Imogen. He touched her arm. His hand lingered just a second longer than it should have.

"Thanks," Imogen said. She smiled at him. There wasn't anything unusual about the way she did it, but abruptly, the pit of my stomach was lined with lead. "You too."

The simple exchange was enough to make me wish the elevator had just kept going down and through the floor, taking me with it. I stood, frozen. The bubbling tension of flirtation fizzed between them.

What was she doing? She didn't like him that way, but she knew I did. She'd told me to hold off so I wouldn't be a rebound. I'd told her he was taking me to a movie and it might even be a date.

So why was she picking imaginary lint off his shoulder and biting her lip like she was waiting for him to lean in and kiss her?

And then he did. A tiny, light peck on the lips, just enough to send panic rushing through my veins.

My skin prickled. This couldn't be right.

The elevator doors clicked and began sliding shut. Instinctively, my hand flew out just in time to stop them, and Imogen turned at the sound. Her face changed only for a moment, but a moment was all I needed. I wasn't the world's greatest faerie, but even I could see the guilt that flashed across her features a split second before her cheerful smile.

No wonder she hadn't texted me back.

My throat closed. In an instant, every floating, happy feeling I'd had was gone. I closed my eyes tight and held them like that for a long second.

I couldn't cry. Not in front of them.

"Hey, Liv!" Imogen said. Her voice was a few shades too bright, but none of the brightness managed to make it onto her face. She was pale. "I ran into Lucas just up the street!"

He grinned and nodded at me, hands in his pockets. He didn't look guilty. But then, he didn't have a reason to be. He hadn't known. He'd probably assumed the movie was just as friends.

And he had probably assumed that because I was nervous and insecure and stupid enough to have taken Imogen's advice when she'd told me to play it cool.

Why had she told me that?

A long, awkward pause stretched out between us. Finally, Lucas rocked back on his heels and said, "Well, I'd better get going."

He looked between Imogen and me, the question vague on his face. "See you guys later?"

Neither of us moved to stop him.

"Sure," Imogen finally said. "See you later."

I couldn't make myself speak.

I watched him go, his tall figure casual and slouching in jeans and a dark green hoodie that almost matched the trees across the street.

Silence hung thick between us. I willed it to grow thicker, to pad the air so heavily that I couldn't hear her say what I already knew.

We stared at each other, each of us waiting for the other one to move first.

I had trusted her. I'd just told her about my parents. She'd told me to leave Lucas alone barely two weeks ago.

My bottom lip began to tremble. I tried to find the words, but nothing would come out.

I could *not* cry in front of her. I couldn't cry until I figured out what the hell was happening here.

As I looked at her, my blood began to simmer.

Her skin flushed. A twisting guilt mangled the air around her. Even from this distance, I felt the way the emotion kneaded at her skin and nudged her every time she dared to breathe. I felt it, and I didn't try to stop it.

The stupid, curious part of myself– the part that some-times checked to see if fire was still hot and knives were still sharp—had to know.

"What happened?" I said. My voice trembled, so I shut up, fast.

Imogen rolled her lips, like she was trying to press exactly the right words out between them.

"We got to talking the other day," she said. Her voice was low, but it travelled across the empty lobby. "He's having a hard time without Aubrey. He said talking to me helped him."

I let the silence settle back around us.

"That's nice, but that's not what I asked," I said finally.

I'd watched Imogen spin words around other people too many times. She was good. She could say all the right things and make people think her decisions were their ideas.

I lowered my glasses to watch her for any signs of a glam-our. I wasn't about to fall for one of her tricks.

"Liv," she said.

I didn't get mad at her often. I didn't get mad at her *ever*. But I could hear my heartbeat in my ears, and I knew she could too.

"I'm sorry," she said again. "We hooked up last night." Hurriedly, she added, "Just kissing. Nothing else, I swear."

Just kissing.

My best friend had been "just kissing" the guy she knew I'd been daydreaming about for months. My best friend had "run into him up the street," and somehow he'd ended up walking her to work. My *best friend* had told me not to say anything to him yet, then turned around and jumped right into his arms.

Fury swirled up in me in a way I hadn't felt in a long time but still recognized as faerie and dangerous. The anger tingled down my arms while pain clenched at my stomach.

No one would ever look at me the way Kyle looked at Elle. And why should they? I wasn't pretty. I wasn't talented. I wasn't Imogen, and I never would be.

But at least I wasn't a liar.

I clenched my fists to stop my fingertips from sparking magic. "Are you dating him?" I said.

My voice came out cooler than I expected. I pressed my tongue hard against the backs of my front teeth and forced myself to hold still.

Imogen's shoulders lifted just barely. "I don't know," she said. "Kind of. Yeah."

I stared at her.

"I was going to tell you," she said. A tiny flare of anger flickered up from her to match my own. "I'm not a jerk. I just wanted to wait for the right time. I didn't want you to freak out like this."

"You didn't want me to freak out," I repeated.

Heat prickled up the back of my neck. She'd always sworn she wasn't into Humdrum guys.

"Of course not," she said. "You're my friend. And no offense, but you kind of freak out over a lot of stuff."

I freaked out? She was the one having daily meltdowns over her sister's wedding. She was the one who'd kept me up until two in the morning panicking the night before her Proctor Exam. She was the one who had *kissed Lucas.*

"Like what?" I snapped. "My best friend lying to me, maybe?"

"Look, I'm sorry," she said. "It's not like you've never done anything wrong in your life. What, you've never kept a secret? You've never lied? Ever?"

She glared at me.

I glared right back. My wonderful day lay in shards around me.

She deflated, just barely. "Look, I know you kind of had a thing for him," she said. "It just happened, okay?"

"Are you going to make it un-happen?" I said.

She bristled. "Excuse me, but you don't own him," she said. "Lucas likes me." She spread out her arms like she was somehow innocent. "I don't know what you want me to do about that."

"I want you have a little respect for me," I said.

"Being the youngest faerie godmother ever doesn't actually mean you get to control everyone's else's romantic decisions, Liv. Sorry. But don't worry about it. Give it a year and you'll be off at your stupid Humdrum college and will have forgotten all about us."

A dozen answers popped into my head, every last one of them worthy of Reginald Feye himself. I took a deep breath, forcing the heat back down into my stomach. I wasn't worried about saying something I'd regret—I was worried I'd say something vicious and never regret it at all.

I'd trusted her. I'd spent the last few days happily trusting her like an idiot and looking forward to something going right in my life, for once.

That was my mistake.

It wouldn't happen again.

CHAPTER EIGHT

Whenever my life had hit a snag, I'd always gone to Imogen for help.

But now she was the problem. Where exactly was I supposed to turn? Lucas was my next best friend after Imogen, and he was so beyond out of the question it wasn't even funny. Talking to my parents or Daniel about my boy troubles was a joke.

I didn't have any other real friends, I realized, staring out my window across the moonlit rooftop garden of the house next door. I had acquaintances and casual friends from school or Glimmering events. I had Elle, who was a former client I happened to like. But none of them were *friends*.

Years ago, Lucas had been special enough that I'd gone to the trouble of hiding the magic around my house and making my family keep their spells to themselves, but not everyone was worth that kind of effort. And it was weird, trying to make friends with other Glims. They all knew who my dad was, and the few times I'd tried bringing one of them home, they'd either spent the whole time asking me what it was like to be *famous* or skulking around after him like I wasn't even there.

Imogen had been my safe place. Imogen had been my protector when people were rude. She'd been the force driving me out to parties and events where I might have a shot at meeting the nice Glims. And she'd been the one I went to when I had guy trouble. Without her, my life was made of holes.

A cloud slipped in front of the full moon, washing the neighbor's garden in darkness. I pushed away from the window.

I needed a faerie godmother. It wasn't enough to *be* one on days like this. But I was the godmother. The only person who could possibly rescue me was—

I froze, frowning. Was it reasonable? Was it right, to trouble her with something as minor-league as this?

Did I care?

I threw a jacket over my arm and headed for the door.

The back of my neck prickled.

In front of me, down a flight of wide, large steps, the Oracle's Fountain burbled. Glassy sheets of water poured over stone blocks. The water seemed to whisper on its way down, as though the Oracle were already dispensing the advice I so desperately needed.

She was my boss's boss's boss, second in authority only to the Faerie Queen. She paid gold pieces in exchange for successfully resolved Stories and was tasked with keeping the city in balance. I didn't quite get how it all worked, or everything her job involved, or even who she was, but I did know this: The Oracle was one of our leaders, and she was wise, all-knowing, and good.

And unlike Queen Amani, she was there to counsel any Glim who needed her.

Imogen had stopped at this Fountain dozens of times when I'd been with her, always to ask for a bottle of enchanted water or a bit of good luck. But I'd never joined her, always preferring to watch.

I was done watching Imogen while life passed me by.

From the corner of my eye, I saw a faint movement. A woman in her thirties, wearing a long brown coat, stood under a tree not far away with her arms wrapped around herself. She glanced at me, eyes narrow and calculating. I smiled and nodded toward the Fountain, and she relaxed, though her arms stayed tight in a hug-like barrier. I was one of us, and that made her feel safer.

I couldn't figure out why, though—it wasn't like Humdrums could see the Oracle's Fountain when it sprang to life anyway.

Even as a Glim, I wouldn't see what she saw when she took her turn, not unless the Oracle allowed me to be part of the encounter.

My phone said 11:58. I put it back in my pocket and watched, counting the seconds in my head. Just as I hit one hundred and three—I'd been counting slow—the Fountain erupted in a magnificent spray of water.

The woman across from me looked my way, ready to fight for her spot, but I gestured her to go ahead. She hurried up to the front of the water and I turned away to give her privacy.

It was hard to turn my back on the Fountain, especially when I heard the woman's low murmuring voice. Even though I'd spoken to the Oracle before, curiosity gnawed at me.

I caught the words *he's Humdrum* and *won't give up*. She sounded impassioned, if quiet. It sounded like Lily wasn't the only one with inter-species relationship drama, and I wished both of them would snap out of it already.

I stepped further away to keep myself from eavesdropping, then entertained myself by counting the windows in the front of the Wishes Fulfilled building and sliding my glasses on and off to make the glamoured top floor disappear and reappear.

A hand tapped my shoulder. Startled, I spun to see the woman in the brown coat. "Your turn," she said, voice low, then walked off into the Portland night, her sensible heels thudding on the sidewalk.

The Fountain seemed to grow as I approached, its glamour shimmering and glowing and making the water sparkle as though stars had tumbled from the sky and into its pools. I didn't need to take off my glasses; even elf-made glass couldn't disguise something the Oracle wanted me to see. Her pale, shadowed face looked out at me from behind a curtain of water, so faintly that it may as well have been my own reflection.

"Olivia Feye," she said, her melodic voice echoing inside my head. "We meet again. I had intended to speak with you. I see you intuited my summons."

That was a new one.

I shoved my hands into my back pockets, then pulled them out again and twisted them together.

"I didn't realize you were going to summon me," I said. "Did you want to talk about my case? Because I've got this one under control, actually."

The Oracle had been the only person to think my last case had gone well. Why would she want to give me advice this time? Maybe she figured lightning couldn't strike twice.

"You do not have it under control," she said. The pale face behind the waterfall remained tranquil. "You were given flawed advice. Your superiors plan to redirect the mermaid's wishes, is that correct?"

She knew it was correct. She was the Oracle. But I nodded.

"That is unwise," she said. "Their intentions are, of course, excellent. But even for the most gifted among us, it is easy to forget our role. What is your job as a faerie godmother?"

"To grant wishes and guide Stories," I said.

That had been our job for centuries: to find likely candidates and guide them through one of the thousands of Stories that had been lived over and over for hundreds of years. The Stories were called "fairy tales" by Humdrums, who hadn't failed to notice the patterns being lived out by their Glimmering neighbors.

"Your role is to resolve Stories, not to pass judgment on them," she said. Her voice was like silk.

That was the rule I had heard over and over, and had never quite known whether to agree with. *But it was the Oracle's mantra,* I reminded myself. It wasn't up to me to agree.

"The godmothers above you did wrong by deciding they and their politics know better than the Story," the Oracle continued. "The Story is always right. This must be remembered."

"If I can redirect her, though, isn't that a new Story?" I said. I pressed my lips together. It was audacious to correct the Oracle. But I couldn't stop the words from escaping. "If she switches from a Little Mermaid Archetype, we'll have to go to Queen Amani. The Faerie Queen has to sign off on all Story changes after a godparent's gotten involved."

Queen Amani was the ultimate ruler of our world. But the Oracle was in charge of Stories. Who had final say?

"There will be no Story change," the Oracle said. "She is a Little Mermaid, and she will remain one. However, I will speak with Queen Amani to ensure things go smoothly. Lily and Evan must be together."

"Or die tragically," I said. "Evan's already engaged to someone."

My teeth snapped back together. What was wrong with me?

"That will be a challenge, but I trust you will overcome it," the Oracle said. She sounded almost wry. "I advise you not to consult with your supervisor, Lorinda, on this. She has done well by me, but convincing her to go against the Sea King will take time, and I should like to hold her blameless in his eyes in any case. And now, I sense you need advice on a personal problem."

My *case* had just become my personal problem—how was I going to explain this to Lorinda? Or the Sea King, for that matter? And why was it okay for all the blame to fall on *me?*

A few silent seconds ticked by. I didn't know how much time the Oracle would give me.

"My best friend just started dating this guy I've been interested in," I said.

A thunderous wave of idiocy washed over me. No one, in the history of ever, had bothered the Oracle with something this stupid.

But she tilted her head, interested.

"Betrayal," she said. She blinked, her black eyes appearing white for an instant beneath the water. "How unfortunate."

I ran one hand along my arm, feeling the goosebumps under my light jacket.

"I don't know what to do about it," I said. "Imogen and I have been friends forever, but I'm so angry at her. How am I supposed to handle this?"

"That does not sound like the action of a friend," the Oracle said.

I wished I could go back in time, just long enough to leave before this conversation started. Why was I asking the Oracle about this? She was a leader of the Glimmering world, not an advice columnist for socially awkward teenagers.

"Imogen's not a bad person," I said. "She's just really selfish sometimes. Maybe I'm overreacting."

Was I, though? She'd made out with a guy she knew I liked. Even for Imogen—reckless, boy-crazy Imogen—that was low. And then she hadn't told me about it. My blood flashed hot.

"I don't want to give up on our friendship over something like this," I said. "But I can't even think about her without wanting to scream."

"Your restraint is admirable," the Oracle said, "if not entirely warranted. Allow me to tell you a little about Imogen Dann."

"You know her?" I said.

"I am the Oracle," she said, and I wanted to kick myself. "I see every Glimmer in this city."

I fell silent and waited.

"Imogen Dann has many secrets," the Oracle said.

Her voice grew quiet and her rippling pale face was still and intense under the curtain of water.

"She cheated on her Proctor Exam, did you know?" She paused to let this sink in, then continued. "She believed she would not be accepted to Institut Glänzen with anything but exemplary scores, so she made sure she got them."

She let out a big sigh, as if she'd been watching Imogen and had felt personally invested.

"It's unfortunate. She would have been accepted on her own merits. As for your friend Lucas, she has had her eye on him for months. She invited him to her house the moment she heard he was unattached. You can see how things went from there. Her attempts at gaining his interest have been especially effective as she's been glamouring him for some time now to see her as being particularly beautiful. Again, she did not need the help, but insecurity certainly breeds overachievement, doesn't it?"

I'd hadn't checked to see if she was glamouring him lately. I'd thought we were all friends. It had never occurred to me to wonder.

"You may try to brush aside her actions out of your friend-ship for her, but deep down you know: He was interested in you. It could have developed into something." Her words faded to almost a whisper. "You were friends with this boy for many years. You know it could have been more."

I rubbed my arm, uncomfortable in a way I couldn't pin down.

"How do you know all that?" I said. Even for the Oracle, that was a lot of detail.

She laughed, a low sound that made the base of my spine prickle.

"It is my business to know," she said, which didn't answer the question.

She gazed out at me from behind the waterfall, still and snow-pale.

"You will not want to take my advice," she said. "But allow me to give it to you anyway. Your supposed friend has betrayed you. Often, the only way to convey the full unacceptability of a behavior is to return it in kind. I have told you secrets about Imogen Dann. You may use them as you wish."

That couldn't be right. But she continued, her words sharp and strong. "Only then can there be balance in your world," she said.

Balance was everything. Balance was the thing the Oracle preserved above all others. Imogen had turned on me; now, I had to turn on her if our relationship—our lives—were to keep the status quo.

Amani wouldn't have given me that advice, I thought.

But then, how did I know what advice she would have given? Every time we'd met, we'd talked about her job or the person who had it out for the Humdrums. It wasn't like we were friends.

Maybe Amani *would* be telling me the same thing right now.

Imogen had done something selfish and cruel, but wouldn't returning the favor make me just as bad? A handful of worn-out truisms about "taking the high road" and "turning the other cheek" flitted through my head, until they were interrupted by the Oracle.

"I look forward to your choices with interest," she said. "You interest me, Olivia Feye."

I frowned. That couldn't be right, either.

"Why?" I said.

"You have a perspective not shared by others in our world," she said. "You enjoy the Humdrums. You are not blinded by your allegiance to the Glimmering world; on the contrary, I believe you could learn to see clearly the advantages and threats the Hums pose to our community. The role of the Humdrums in our city has been called into question of late."

"I know," I said. The Oracle's faint rippling eyebrows knitted together. "I've heard things have been going on with the... the Humdrums," I said.

I bit my lip. How much could I tell her?

"I've heard rumors that some people don't want them in the city," I said.

She watched me closely, shadowed eyes dark but unmoving.

"Indeed," she said after a moment. "You understand more than I anticipated. As I said, I watch you with interest."

And with that unnerving pronouncement, her face rippled away out of sight. The Fountain went back to being a fountain, full of nothing but cold rushing water and the faint reflections of street lamps.

CHAPTER NINE

The next afternoon, I skipped final period. I had to think, and I couldn't do it in the crushing halls of a high school where I risked running into my former best friend at any moment.

The bell rang when I pushed open the door to Pumpkin Spice. But that was the only noise. The café was quiet. The only person here was a college-aged wizard who worked weekdays when Elle was at school. He sat behind the counter with a textbook propped on his lap.

He jumped up as soon as I reached the counter. "What can I get for you?" he said.

I glanced at the menu behind him, written in glittering gold on a background the dark green of a pumpkin stem.

"Chili cocoa," I said.

"You got it."

I took my drink to a small table and waited. A drizzly rain started outside.

I couldn't get the Oracle out of my head. She knew something, that was for sure, and I didn't know if she'd learned it from Queen Amani or on her own.

But she wouldn't need to learn it from Queen Amani. If she was watching our lives down to the details of Imogen's Proctor Exam and my opinions on Humdrums, nothing could be hidden from her.

If that was the case, then she already knew who was attacking the Humdrums, and she wasn't telling.

Any other day, I might have shivered and worried about the fate of the Humdrum world. But today, Imogen burned through my thoughts, turning everything else to smoke.

Tendrils of rage snaked down the veins in my arms and made my hands hot enough that my cocoa gave off a curl of steam every time I touched it. If the Oracle was right, and Imogen had cheated, I knew all I needed to know.

Anyone who could cheat on an exam and their best friend all in the same month wasn't worth my time.

Stop thinking about her, Feye, I mentally ordered. *Move on with your life.*

How could she be so stupid? It wasn't like cheating on a Proctor Exam wouldn't have consequences. If word got out, she'd never make it into any school, let alone Institut Glänzen. She'd probably lose her job. And Imogen would care about something like that.

But maybe she didn't care. Maybe she just got off on the thrill of lying to people.

I pulled out my phone to text her. My fingers were like hammers on the screen.

Olivia: What is wrong with you?!

I hit Send. Immediately, a sense of regret flooded me. I was stupid for even wasting my time.

My cocoa steamed.

The bell rang and I looked up to see Elle. She shook her head, tossing damp blond hair out of her eyes, and called across to the guy behind the counter, "Hey, toss a tray of scones in the oven to warm, would you?"

Then she saw me. She slid into the chair opposite me without waiting for an invitation.

"What's wrong with you?"

That was Elle, always cutting straight to the chase.

I couldn't get the words to form. Too many of them clamored around my mind and in my mouth. Stringing them into sentences was impossible.

"What?" Elle said. The spot between her eyebrows creased. "Hey, are you okay?"

No, I was not okay. Nothing about anything was okay.

"Hello?"

"Imogen and Lucas are dating," I blurted.

And then the back of my throat started closing up and a hot prickling started behind my eyes. I stared at my cup. I was *not* going to burst into tears in the middle of this café like a child.

"Shit," Elle said.

It was the right answer. I laughed. The prickling faded.

"Are you serious?" she said. Her eyes were like two cups of steaming coffee, round and brown and vaguely caffeinated. "When? What happened?"

I opened my mouth to tell her, but she glanced up at the pumpkin-shaped clock on the wall behind the counter and interrupted.

"Listen, it's almost time for the after-school rush," she said. "Come talk to me while I work. Logan's getting off in five minutes and Cortney's going to be late today."

"You want some help?" I said. "Unless I'd be in the way."

"I would freaking love some help," she said. "Cortney's at the eye doctor and who knows how long that's going to take."

I stood and followed Elle to the counter.

"She getting glasses?"

"Who knows," Elle said. "She says her vision gets blurry when she reads, but I'm not totally sure she *can* read."

Despite her tone, I felt the begrudging affection underneath. Cortney and Elle were stepsisters, and Elle had come to that union kicking and screaming. But they'd gotten used to each other.

Elle led me behind the counter and handed me an orange apron to tie around my waist. She pointed around at the bottles and dark green canisters that littered the counter.

"Sorry, I swear we'll talk through this in a minute. Right now, listen up. Italian syrups, seltzer, carbonated Fountain of Youth water, cream, fairy dust," she said, her finger jabbing with each new item. "The mini fridge under the counter has apple spritzers from a Tree of Life. Nonalcoholic, obviously, but I have a policy that we only sell one of those per customer per day. Two in a row would probably land you in the hospital."

The number of bottles overwhelmed me, and I was glad. Being overwhelmed by anything that wasn't Imogen or the Humdrum attacker was a relief.

Elle pulled a crystal bottle with a flame-colored stopper out from behind a stack of paper cups.

"Dragon tears," she said. "I use them for keeping drinks hot, but careful or you'll get burned."

She directed me to a laminated card that listed recipes and instructions for Italian sodas, fairy dust sodas, and mocktails.

"You put dragon tears in fairy dust sodas?" I said.

"Gross, right?" she said. "That's what I thought until I tried it."

The bell on the door jingled as two girls came in with backpacks. I got their muffins out of the glass-fronted case while Elle whipped up their drinks. Once they were sitting at one of the tables, Elle leaned against the counter.

"So," she said. "Imogen and Lucas."

I explained the whole story as quickly as I could. I liked him, he seemed to like me, he got dumped, Imogen said to wait, and then—

"They were right there in the lobby, and he kissed her."

Elle winced. "Ouch," she said.

"Yeah, and then I asked her—"

I was interrupted by customers, who wanted mochas and blueberry sodas. I made the soda while Elle kept one eye on me.

"So I asked her—"

And then we were interrupted again, and it was another hour before I could finish the sentence. I couldn't believe how crazy it felt behind the counter, or how cool Elle was in the middle of it. She whipped out drinks and joked with customers and calculated change in her head like there was nothing to it. Meanwhile, I kept reading the wrong lines on the recipe card and had to re-make someone's drink twice because I couldn't keep the fairy dust from clumping as soon as it hit the seltzer.

Finally, the place was full of contented Glimmers sipping beverages and nibbling on pastries.

Elle turned to me.

"Okay, so you asked her about it."

"And she said he'd been telling her all about Aubrey and that talking to her 'helped him.'"

The words alone made me want to gag. How cloying could she get?

"I'm sure her glamours didn't hurt," I muttered.

"She'd been glamouring him?"

I thought about pointing out that Elle wasn't one to talk, seeing as how, once she'd learned about her Glimmering heritage, she'd spent the next several months manipulating everyone she knew with charms. Unlike Imogen, though, Elle had learned her lesson.

"Probably for a while," I said. "And then they hooked up."

Elle's eyes flashed.

"Like, how hooked up?" Elle said.

"Just kissing," I said quickly.

"But still," Elle said.

We fell silent. At least I didn't have to explain to her what was wrong about all this. She'd grasped in seconds what Imogen probably still hadn't figured out.

The bell on the door rang and I looked up, poised to jump back into action. But it was just Cortney, Elle's Humdrum stepsister, whose normally sky-high enthusiasm had doubled since she'd learned about the Glimmering world. She came behind the counter and put on an apron.

"Olivia!" she said, as soon as she saw me. "Oh my gosh, hi! How are you?"

Everything that came out of her mouth was about twice as enthusiastic as it needed to be.

"I'm good," I lied. "Just helping out for a couple of hours."

"Super fab!"

She leaned in to give me a quick hug and then went back into the larger room, where she started clearing drinks and napkins from tables. She stopped to flirt with a couple of guys sitting near the window.

"She is such a child," Elle said. "Okay, so what are you going to do about all this?"

I wiped a dribble of syrup off the counter.

"I already went to the Oracle," I said.

"Wow," she said. "Gutsy move, kid."

"I'm an idiot," I said. "It was ridiculous. I know."

"Not ridiculous, just bold. What'd she say?"

I let out a long sigh. The air seemed more than ready to escape from me, and I didn't blame it. I wished I could run away from the thoughts fizzing in my head, too.

"She seems kind of… revenge-y," I said. "She told me some stuff about Imogen and said I could do whatever I wanted with it."

Elle's eyebrows furrowed.

"Weird."

For some reason, I didn't like Elle saying exactly what I'd been thinking.

"She must have a reason," I said.

"I guess," Elle said. "That's terrible advice, though."

"She can't give terrible advice," I said. "She's the Oracle."

Elle hadn't even been in our world a year yet. No one who'd been around longer would say something like that and be serious.

And yet.

"Are you sure you didn't, like, misunderstand her or something?" Elle said.

"Maybe?" I said.

I tapped the counter with my fingernail. It made a satisfying clicking sound and sent a tiny jolt of sensation up my hand with every tap.

"No," I corrected. "She was pretty clear. But it makes sense, when you think about it. Her job is to keep balance in our world."

"Like, an eye for an eye kind of stuff?" Elle said. "That's messed up."

"That's what holds our world together," I said.

My tone was too sharp, and she held her hands up.

"Hey, I'm not arguing," she said. "It's your world. I still don't get how half of this works. It's just weird."

Cortney came back behind the counter, a stack of cups balanced in each hand. She disappeared behind the curtain that led to the small kitchen.

My phone buzzed. My stomach twisted.

Imogen.

I reached for it, wishing I hadn't texted her.

Amani: Our friend Eris just released a swarm of fairies into a brand-new Humdrum apartment complex. Just fyi.

Not Imogen, then. But also not good news.

Technically, the horrible little creatures were called hex moths, but everyone called them fairies since they looked so much like my race. They had our human figures and the wings our species had lost to evolution thousands of years ago, but they were nothing but pests, half as bright as most household pets and a thousand times as mean. As far as I was concerned, the dust that constantly fell from their wings was the only good thing about them. And their bites were nasty. A whole swarm of them in a building of Humdrums could mean disaster.

"What's wrong?" Elle said.

"I just got a Glimmering news alert," I said, which was not exactly a lie. "A fairy swarm just invaded some apartments downtown."

"Keep tearing down old buildings and they have to find a new home, same as anyone," she said. "Just another reason for people to be upset about all the historic homes people are destroying out of capitalistic greed."

And then she was off, talking about gentrification and social stratification and evil corporations.

As she talked, I sent Amani a quick message back.

Olivia: Thanks for the update. I'll keep an ear out for any gossip. Any news on who we're dealing with?

Calling the two of us "we" felt weird, but I kept it in and hit Send. Amani wanted me, after all. She wouldn't get offended or think I was getting above myself.

Probably.

We might not exactly be friends, but our meeting in the garden had been nice. The garden itself was amazing, and I'd liked talking with Amani.

And then, like an idiot, I'd gone and suggested that Imogen should be her heir. Freaking Imogen. I shouldn't have even mentioned Imogen, let alone suggested she—of all the dishonest, unreliable people—should be selected as the leader of the Glimmering world.

Imagining her as our queen made my ears feel hot. I felt my magic fizz around my fingertips. A world where she was in charge would be a disaster, and if that happened, it would be all my fault.

Elle snapped her fingers.

"Yo," she said. "You're not listening."

"Sorry," I said. "I started thinking about Imogen."

She pursed her lips. "Guys aren't everything," she said. "You changed my life. I'd like to see Imogen do that."

I glanced up to see a new customer coming through the door. It wasn't about changing lives or even guys. It was about so much more than that: lying and honesty and what it meant to be friends and the way I'd always let Imogen walk all over me.

Silently, I promised myself I would do my best on this Lily case, if only to prove to Amani and myself that I could take life by the reins just as much as Imogen did. I could have even been queen if I'd wanted to. Imogen wasn't that great by comparison. After all, she wasn't the youngest godmother in a hundred years. And she was, apparently, a pathological liar.

I'd have to find a way to bring that up to Queen Amani next time we spoke.

I didn't want to be queen. I just didn't want *her* to have a shot.

CHAPTER TEN

It was six in the morning and already the sun burned through my thin T-shirt as I knelt on the banks of the river. It was secluded here, but I'd still thrown a Humdrum shield up. Anyone who wandered by my pocket of the waterfront would think the high grasses that surrounded my little patch of sand were too tall and itchy, or they'd suddenly remember they forgot to grab a bag to clean up after their dog.

Lily and I had finally found a time that worked for both of us. I'd called her through a seashell a few days ago and sent a message in a bottle last night to confirm our appointment. Now, I sat cross-legged on the banks of the river and waited. The water rippled, each wave a dark steely blue and crowned with pale light.

The Oracle's comments still didn't make sense, I thought as I watched the river flow past. Her advice to turn around and betray Imogen, on the other hand, kind of did. That was what balance looked like, and balance was important. The words had still seemed strange coming from someone as wise and good as the Oracle, but maybe that just suggested I didn't quite understand what "wise" included.

At any rate, I couldn't deny the temptation. I couldn't think about Imogen without my stomach flipping over and twisting into knots.

I picked a fat blade of grass and slowly tore it into long strips.

Maybe Imogen did deserve to have her secrets spilled. She hadn't just hurt me—she'd done real wrong. She had cheated on her Proctor Exam.

I didn't want to believe Imogen would do that, but I couldn't lie to myself. She'd always cheated at cards. Even when she'd winked to let me know she was cheating, I could always see the faint glamour that meant she was trying to trick me into thinking her devious behavior was charming, and I'd always played along because she was my best friend and best friends let each other get away with stuff.

I threw the ruined blade of grass into the water. The green strands clung to the surface like it was sticky, and then they were caught in a slow eddy and carried away.

Maybe it was time to stop letting Imogen get away with stuff. Maybe our friendship was nothing but a series of bad habits, and she'd only been my friend all these years because she knew I'd put up with anything.

Maybe none of it had been real.

The water ten feet in front of me rippled and the auburn crown of a head drifted toward me like a bubble on the river's surface. Lily breached a moment later, her white skin glowing in the new morning light.

Her pearly smile dazzled me.

"You must be Olivia," she said.

She swam forward to take my outstretched hand. The water here dropped off abruptly, which was why I'd chosen this site. If she propped her elbows on the ground to face me, the water was still deep enough that her tail could stay submerged as it stretched out behind her. Her hand felt small, with delicate bones that could have belonged to a fish or a bird or some other flighty creature.

I bowed my head low over her hand, the closest thing to a curtsy I could approximate from a seating position. "Your Royal Highness," I said.

She smiled at me and twitched an iridescent green fin.

"You can call me Lily," she said.

I'd met more than a few princesses in my day who bristled at anything less than the full pomp and circumstance their—

usually outdated—titles afforded them. But Lily didn't carry herself like other princesses did. She gazed at me, eyes rapt and alert. Her red hair cascaded down her shoulders and into the water. It was streaked with green seaweed and knotted with seashells and bits of sea glass.

"Thanks for meeting me here," I said.

"Good excuse to come up to the city," she said. She put her chin in her hands. "Father is not fond of me spending time in town."

"I heard," I said. "So, you're in love with someone named Evan."

Much as I wanted to sit and chat with her, it was daylight in the middle of the city and I was in conversation with a mermaid. We didn't have time for niceties.

Lily sighed, her gaze growing soft and dreamy.

"Yes, Evan," she said. "He is magnificent."

"About that," I said. "He's engaged."

I waited for her eyes to sharpen and her strangely wild face to broadcast dismay, but it didn't happen. Instead, she pursed her lips a little and nodded, as though the presence of another woman's prior claim was nothing more than a sad inconvenience.

"He has a fiancée," I said.

She shifted, moving her chin from one cupped hand to the other.

"It's very unfortunate," she said. "I wish things were easier. I know this will make your job more challenging."

"I'm not really worried about my job," I said.

"You're worried about the other girl," Lily said. "Yes. I'm trying not to feel too bad for her. She'll be happier in the long run, you know. Evan can't possibly be her true love. He's mine, and we each only get one. But of course you know that."

Her voice lilted, each word falling on a new note like every sentence was a song.

As far as I was concerned, "true love" was mostly a figment of imagination, hormones, and choice. Anyone who thought differently had turned their brains over to cartoon fairy tales. But no self-respecting godmother could say that.

Especially not a godmother who'd stopped talking to her best friend over a guy.

"How sure are you that he's your 'true love?'" I said instead.

She sighed. A mosquito hummed around her face and she waved it dreamily off like it was a butterfly.

"Completely sure. I just *know*," she said. "I looked into his eyes and I saw forever in them, laid out like a path designed for two people to walk side by side."

A gagging noise made its way out of my throat and I turned it into a cough. Her face was so earnest that I wanted to laugh just to dissipate the uncomfortable itch that had taken root in my stomach.

"No kidding," I said.

"It's the most remarkable thing," she said. "And once you've seen it, you know. There will never be another choice for you."

She sighed and her arm dropped to the sandy ground, her head falling with it to rest as though her arm were a pillow.

"He's so beautiful, faerie godmother."

"Olivia," I said.

"And you're going to make him mine," she said, jumping back up.

Her eyes glittered. I couldn't tell if it was enthusiasm or insanity looking out.

I held up a hand.

"I can't actually make anyone yours," I said. "I'm forbidden from using love potions or manipulating people like that."

This was a flat-out lie. Love potions just took a lot of paperwork, and I wasn't about to waste them on a girl whose "true love" already had a fiancée—and whose dad would make my life a living hell if I let his daughter throw her life away on some tailless dude.

Lily reached out and touched my wrist. Her skin was wet and cool.

"Evan and I don't need anything like that," she said. "All I need is legs. He thinks I'm training for a swimming contest, but even love can't blind him forever to the fact that he only sees me in the water. Oh, and I need a phone number. He

113

keeps asking for my number so he can 'text' me, but I don't know what that means."

And this was supposed to be the foundation for a healthy relationship.

"You have to help me," Lily said.

She squeezed my arm, and her green eyes were wide and earnest.

"I can't let him marry her," she said. "I can't let him marry another woman. He doesn't realize what we could have. He doesn't understand how much I care about him. If he marries her, I've lost him forever."

Tears rose up and pooled in the corners of her wide eyes, hovering at the edges and threatening to fall. She looked so much sadder than anyone should have been able to look over something so unreasonable.

"I can't think about them together," she said.

With no warning, my throat closed up. I swallowed, hard, and pushed back the thought of Imogen and Lucas.

I saw them together every time I closed my eyes. I kept picturing her holding his hand, talking about his day, kissing him —doing all the things I'd meant to do. I'd been assuming Lily was just a melodramatic mermaid. But maybe she was just another girl whose guy didn't realize she existed.

Maybe the Oracle was right. Was it so impossible that Lily and Evan were meant to be together? It wasn't like I knew enough about godparenting to say. After all, the success of my last case had been a fluke.

"I'm not really a fairy godmother," I said. It seemed important that she knew this. "I'm just working this job so I can pay for college."

Her confused frown shouldn't have surprised me. Mermaids didn't age the way the rest of us did. They looked perpetually seventeen for most of their adult lives, and "higher education" was mostly theoretical down where kelp farming, sea witchery, singing sailors to their deaths, and floating around aimlessly were the major occupations.

"Are you filling in for someone?" she said finally. "I was told you were my godmother."

"I am your godmother," I said. "But I'm an intern."

She didn't seem to know what this meant, either. Getting her on land was going to be more than a matter of legs. She needed a full crash course in humanity.

"An intern is someone who works to get experience," I said. "It means I don't have a lot of experience yet. To be honest, I probably never will. I'm not making this a career or anything."

Her shimmering tail spasmed like she was trying to decide whether to swim away or not.

"I'm going to try to help you," I said.

I looked past her at the water glittering in the morning light.

"Can I be honest with you?"

"Please do," Lily said. "Honesty is a good foundation for a partnership like ours."

"I think this is a bad idea," I said. "Like, a really bad idea. It's wrong to try to steal someone away when they're already with someone who cares about them."

Imogen flitted across my thoughts and the back of my neck flushed hot.

"But I've been told by someone who knows about these things that you're supposed to have this chance," I said. "And in my last case, my client knew what was best for her, so maybe that's true for you."

"It is," Lily said.

"I'll make you a deal," I said. "I think you're doing the wrong thing. But I also think it's your right to try. So I'm going to do my best to give you and Evan a chance, and what you guys do with that chance is up to you."

What would have happened if Lucas and I had tried? If I'd been the one to thoughtlessly invite him over right off instead of being a real friend and respecting his space, would I be exploring the city with him right now instead of sitting on the banks of a river, talking to a lovesick mermaid?

"A chance is all we need," Lily said.

She pressed her hands firmly on the ground and pressed herself up, scooting until she sat in the shallows with her tail twitching in the water like an anxious cat's.

"He's my soulmate. I know he'll choose me."

This mermaid was willing to grow legs and leave her whole world behind for her human—maybe that was a better love than the one he had now. The thought still made my stomach churn.

I drew my knees to my chin and watched her. "You're going to have to give me a while to figure this out," I said. "There are some people who really don't want me to make you human."

"My father," she said. "He's objected since the beginning."

"And my boss," I said. "Who your dad's been talking to."

"So the world is against me," she said.

I couldn't tell whether she thought of this as a hardship or an interesting challenge. I sighed.

"Pretty much," I said. "Everyone except the Oracle. She's in charge of Stories around here, and that's why I'm still talking to you."

"Then please move as quickly as you can," Lily said. "Every day away from him is a day closer to losing him. That can't happen."

Unfortunately, it could. It was one of the main ways a Little Mermaid trope ended. But I wrapped my arms around my knees and clutched them to me, thinking hard.

The legs were the problem.

"How much money do you have?"

She tucked a tiny shell-studded braid behind her ear. "Not much," she said. "I had to use my own coins for this, you understand. I've already given Wishes Fulfilled almost everything I had." Her delicate eyebrows drew together. "There aren't extra fees, are there?"

"The problem is, you need legs," I said. "And legs are going to be expensive. We have to hire consultants for transformations this major, and transformation specialists can pretty much charge whatever they want."

Her face fell. Her bottom lip trembled, and I held out a hand, trying to will her tears to stay in her eyes.

Lorinda would never sign off on using company funds. And King Pacifica would never hand over the kind of gold we needed.

"I think I have an idea," I said. "It has to wait till this weekend, though. Can you meet me in Newport on Saturday?"

She leaned forward. "I can do anything."

My phone buzzed in my pocket, making me jump. I shifted to get it out.

"Sorry—this might be my boss," I said.

Tabitha had hinted she might need me to run some errands in town before I came into the office later this morning. But it wasn't Tabitha.

Imogen: Can we talk?

I took a long, steadying breath before replying.

Olivia: Are you still with Lucas?

Only a few seconds passed while I watched the darkened screen of my phone. And then the light went on and the phone buzzed again.

Imogen: I'm really stressed right now and he helps me. Can we please talk in person?

That was a yes. And, once again, it was all about her.

I stared at the phone until the words swam in front of my eyes before clicking the screen off.

I didn't want to talk to her.

I wanted to swear at her.

I wanted to scream at her.

I wanted to say every horrible thing I could think of, and then I wanted to repeat each of them slowly, just so I could be sure she got the message.

Cruel words should have come easily. I'd lived with my dad long enough to learn them all. But Imogen had already screwed me over enough this week. She didn't get to turn me into Reginald Feye, too.

I turned back to Lily, who stared at me with breathless anticipation. I swallowed hard. My eyes prickled again, but I blinked the feeling back before Lily could notice anything was wrong.

"Good," I said. I cleared my throat. "Because this could get a little tricky."

CHAPTER ELEVEN

A few years back, my parents had noticed I wasn't as enthusiastic about the Glimmering world as they thought I should
be, and had enrolled me in a Magical Enrichment Program for
Sublunary Youth. The whole thing had been a summer-long
headache, and I'd been convinced I'd never get anything out of
it.

It was nice to be proved wrong.

Daniel and I flew to Newport on an old magic carpet that
had spent the last few years rolled up in the corner of our attic.
I didn't mention the carpet or the destination to either of my
parents. They still didn't dare let me take the car to the other
side of Portland without a responsible adult in the passenger
seat. There was no way they'd be okay with my flying a magic

carpet to the coast, and they'd be doubly not okay with my taking Daniel as my co-pilot.

Mom had threatened Daniel this morning with a whole list of chores if he didn't stop "moping around the house like a ghost off its Prozac." He'd decided helping me out was better than changing out of his black turtleneck and putting on a smile. And that was lucky, because the huge carpet steered a lot better with two people enchanting the way.

Now that we were safe inside the colorful coastal aquarium, he rocked back on his heels with his hands in his pockets.

"I'm headed to the octopus," he said.

I waved, though he'd already darted off, a slim shadow ducking between happy tourist families. I turned back to the displays. I vaguely remembered the woman I needed to see from a Magical Enrichment Program field trip, but I had no idea how to reach her. I wasn't sure where I'd find what I was looking for, only that I'd know it if I saw it.

That was the idea, anyway. That was the idea with a lot of things in our world, usually because the person giving directions was under the impression that everything Glimmering was somehow better and more thrilling if it was a surprise.

Glims seemed to have this idea that Humdrums were boring and obvious. But, I mused as I wandered past tanks of bug-eyed fish, the Humdrums were the ones who'd managed to survive the elements and build entire civilizations without a smidgen of magic to help them along. Didn't that make *them* the extraordinary ones?

I glanced at the JinxNet page I'd saved to my phone. The only available picture was a tiny thumbnail, but it was enough to guide my search. I walked through the aquarium, my gaze skimming every tank and pausing whenever I caught a flash of gold. The biggest flash made me stop.

The tank held one of the fattest fish I'd ever seen. Its scales glinted in the tank's mellow light, but I knew it wasn't a koi or goldfish or anything else. It certainly wasn't anything that could be found in Oregon's coastal waters.

The fat yellow-gold fish swam lazily back and forth. I leaned in toward the tank until the tip of my nose touched the smooth cool glass.

"I wish to see the Sea Witch," I whispered.

One of the fish's eyes turned sharply toward me. The fin on top of its body twitched.

Do you have an appointment? the fish asked through the glass, in a voice so distant it might as well have been inside my own head. Bubbles rose from its mouth and streamed to the top of the tank.

"No," I whispered. "I'm a drop-in. The website said it was okay."

You're in luck. The Witch has had a slow day. She'll see you in ten minutes, the fish said. Its soft voice was polite. *Please feel welcome to view the exhibits while you wait.*

It gestured around the room with one of its side fins, then returned to pacing the tank.

For a Wish Fish, it seemed awfully like a receptionist. But then, for a faerie godmother, I looked a lot like a high schooler. Our appearances were just a couple of convenient lies that let us get by in this blended world.

I wiggled my fingers in a discreet wave and went back to walking around the colorful room, jerking my head up whenever someone new entered the space.

My phone buzzed.

Amani: Anything new?

Every time I saw her name on my phone, I jumped a little. It was still too weird.

Olivia: No, things are quiet.

In the tank next to me, a fat gray fish floated by. It made eye contact for a moment before moving along.

I felt her arrive before I saw her. It was hard to pin down what exactly had changed, but the moment she entered the room, something was different. My head jerked up and my eyes met hers; they were dark and piercing and her gaze went straight through me.

The witch walked across the room with purposeful steps, wiping her hands on a worn-out white towel hooked through her belt loop. She wore a boring dark blue polo shirt and equally boring khakis. Her dark ponytail frizzed out the back of her blue baseball cap. She looked like just some woman in her forties who kept fish alive for a living. But the air around her felt thick and liquid. When I glanced discreetly over my glasses, I saw translucent bluish-green eels and a single fat octopus floating around her like ghosts caught in a lazy green vortex.

"Are you here for the volunteer orientation?" she said.

I shook my head, and she frowned a little and said, "They're late. But what did I expect? No water sprite has ever showed up on time."

Sprites were famously flaky. Either they declared allegiance to a leader like the Oracle and became almost mindlessly devoted allies, or they flitted around with the attention span of a butterfly. There was no in-between.

"I'm a drop-in," I said. "I need a wish granted and you seem like the only one who can help."

She put her hands on her hips and looked down at me, her thick, dark eyebrows turning her otherwise mild gaze thunderous.

"What kind of wish?" she said.

"I'm a faerie godmother at Wishes Fulfilled in Portland," I said. "I've got a mermaid client who needs legs."

"Don't you have enchantments for that?" she said.

"We do," I said. "Unfortunately, my supervisor can't endorse one. She's trying to keep a good relationship with King Neptune Pacifica, so this needs to be all on my authority. I don't have the skills to work up a transformation spell on that scale."

Her eyes narrowed. "Why is King Neptune involved?" she asked.

That was the big question, and I had a feeling she wouldn't help me once she'd heard the answer.

"He's my client's dad," I said. "And he's not okay with her becoming human. Like, *really* not okay."

"Nor should he be," she said. "It's not bad for a jaunt." She gestured down at her own legs, which, I realized, were probably not always part of her body. "But I don't know why anyone would choose land as a permanent residence. If the gravity doesn't get you, you'll choke to death on all the air."

She kept staring down at me, blinking slowly every few seconds like she had all the time in the world.

"Say I give her legs," she said. "What's in it for me?"

I held out my hand and flipped it so my palm was facing the ground, then flipped it back up, envisioning the bag of coins

I'd carefully magicked into safe storage in my energy field this morning. The bag shimmered into my palm, small but heavy.

"My client can offer gold," I said. "It's not much, but she can add to it after she's been human long enough to get a job."

The corner of the Sea Witch's mouth twitched. I fought to hold still under her gaze. Had I offered too little? Too much?

"That's an interesting offer," she said. "But I don't need gold."

My heart sank. It was all I had. Normally, I might try to barter magic skills—my green thumb to revive her garden, maybe, or a small charm to bring her luck. But she was the Sea Witch. Not a sea witch, but *the* Sea Witch, the ultimate authority on magic in this region of the Pacific Ocean.

I had nothing else to offer.

"I've heard King Neptune's daughters have pretty voices," she said.

I shrugged. "I hear all mer-people do."

"Theirs especially," she said. "Listen, I'll make the girl a trade. I'll give her legs if she'll give me her voice."

I took a small step back. Lily wanted Evan, but I didn't know how high a price she'd be willing to pay. I couldn't agree to something of that magnitude without her permission, that was for sure.

The Sea Witch reached up and tightened her ponytail.

"I'm not going to *take* it," she said. "Don't look so worried. I just figure, what is this, a Little Mermaid trope?"

I nodded, and she said, "That's what I thought. It seems poetic that the Sea Witch should ask for the girl's voice, and I just so happen to need a narrator for a new display on crustaceans we're putting up. I'll enchant a copy of her voice for safekeeping and narration, and she can keep the real thing. It'll be a fair trade. What do you say?"

"Yes," I said, almost before she'd finished speaking. Hope rose up in me like a bubble out of the Wish Fish's mouth. "Yes, I think she'll agree to that."

"Fantastic," the Witch said. "What do you say I meet you later this afternoon after I get off? There are some little islands off the coast of the state park up north. You'll know them when you see them. Meet me there at six."

CHAPTER TWELVE

An enormous wave crashed against the ground a foot from where I stood. I threw out my arms for balance and stepped back, though it didn't do much good. The island the Sea Witch had directed us to was hardly an island at all. At best, it was a large rock jutting out of the sea. A thick, briny haze of magic rose from it. This particular rock had been glamoured so we'd look like shifting mist if someone happened to glance where we stood, but it didn't offer much by way of comfort.

Daniel crouched at the water's edge, in serious conversation with my client. I wasn't sure whether it was her fascinating repartee or the fact that she had only the tiniest of seashells for clothing, but I wasn't about to argue with him; he'd helped get me and the magic carpet here in one piece despite the strong breeze blowing in off the water. Lily had arrived at the island before us, no doubt eager to get her dreams quickly on their way to reality.

My impression of the Sea Witch had been of someone who liked to make an appearance, but her head poked out of the water as silently as a sea lion's. I only saw her because she happened to come up right beside Lily. Her wild curls were tamed by the water into sleek black coils that dripped down her bare shoulders.

She raised an arm and beckoned me closer. I took a step down toward them, careful to crouch and brace myself with my free hand against the slick stone.

"You must be the Sea King's daughter," the Witch said to Lily, not bothering to say hello.

Lily bobbed in the water and bowed her head.

"Princess Lily Pacifica, ma'am."

The Sea Witch didn't return the aquatic curtsy.

"I heard you have a voice," she said.

"So they tell me, Your Ladyship," Lily said.

It occurred to me that the Sea Witch might have been an even bigger deal than I thought, if Lily was calling her Your Ladyship. There were too many things I didn't know about my own world. And if I was this clueless about my own community, how much was I missing about the Humdrum world? I couldn't get there fast enough.

The Sea Witch grabbed Lily's chin and turned her face this way and that, analyzing her for Titania knew what.

"The faerie gave you my price?" she demanded.

"Yes, ma'am," Lily said. "I'm happy to pay it."

"As well you should be," the Witch said. "I'm a saint for letting you off so cheaply."

Daniel laughed, and the Sea Witch's eyes darted to fix on his face. She stared at him for a moment, then gave him a sharp nod like she approved of whatever she saw.

She reached into her thick hair and dug around for a moment as though trying to find an elusive itch. After a moment, her fingers reappeared, holding a tiny old-fashioned cassette recorder dotted with tiny barnacles.

"You should teach Olivia that trick," Daniel said. "Her hair's frizzy enough."

I wanted to kick him to make him shut up, but I couldn't without risking slipping off into the water. Another wave crashed behind us, sending frothy white foam around the rock to lap around the Witch's and Lily's shoulders.

The Witch held the cassette recorder up to Lily's mouth.

"Speak," she said.

"What should I say?" Lily said.

"Tell me why you want legs," said the Witch. "That should matter enough to you for the spell to take."

A dreamy expression I was starting to recognize stole across Lily's face.

"I want legs so I can be with my one true love," she said. "He is my soulmate and I'm ready to give up everything for the chance of a life in his arms."

Daniel whipped his head around to me and muttered, "Are you kidding me?"

I couldn't hear him over Lily's voice and the waves crashing around us, but I could read his lips. I didn't have a good answer. I thought the same thing every other time she opened her mouth.

The Sea Witch didn't seem perturbed. She watched the cassette tape spin in the recorder.

"Evan is the man I was put on this earth to love," Lily said. "He only needs a chance to be with me in order to realize our true potential together. And I need legs, because he's a human and a Hum, and he can't know about our world until we're to be married."

That was the law. Glims and Hums lived in different worlds. Only a true commitment like marriage—or a pressing need to know, like becoming President and inheriting a relationship with the highest Glimmering Councils—was considered a good enough reason to let the worlds touch.

I had always liked that law. I didn't want my Humdrum friends to know I was magical. I wondered if I'd feel differently in Lily's place, unable to tell my "true love" who I really was. I'd always been glad to keep that particular secret from Lucas.

Not that he was my true love. It was obnoxious how often I had to remind myself.

Marrying Evan, though, had seemed to be Lily's plan from the beginning. From the way she talked, I got the feeling she thought they'd be on their honeymoon in a week.

I'd be lucky if I had her walking a straight line by then.

"Sing a scale for me," the Witch said. "La-la-las."

Lily complied, trilling out a crystalline song that made the hair on my arms stand up. For the first time, I understood why there were legends of sailors jumping overboard to chase the mermaids' music.

The Witch clicked a button on her tape recorder and the wheels stopped spinning. She tucked it back in her hair, where it disappeared in the folds of her heavy curls.

"That's plenty," she said. She touched Lily's cheek and pursed her lips. "You sure about this?" she said. "Being human can be nasty business."

"I'm sure," Lily said. Her eyes glowed with a fire that toed the line between fervor and mania. "Evan is my life. I would do anything for him."

"You might have to," the Witch said.

She reached back into her hair and produced a small crystal bottle filled with what looked like glittering blue sand.

"Sprinkle this on your tail and tongue," she said. "Make sure you're somewhere private, because it'll hurt like hell. Nothing to be done about that, but the pain's gone as quickly as it comes. It used to stick around like you were walking on knives. Thank Poseidon magic's progressed in the last few years."

She handed the bottle to Lily, who took it as though it were made of diamonds.

"Thank you, Your Ladyship!" Lily said. "I hope you know what this means to me."

"It was a fair trade," the Witch said.

She patted her hair, where the tape recorder lay hidden.

"You just make sure this is what you want," she said. "You have to truly believe you're meant to be human. You've got to rely on your belief or it will all go wrong and you'll end up with scaly legs or a tail with toes or the Kraken knows what."

Concern crossed Lily's features, but it was gone in a blink. She clutched the bottle to her heart.

The Witch turned to me and added, "Good luck."

She offered Daniel a smile and a wink, and then she was gone without another word. Her eel's tail slapped the water behind her as she dove into the Pacific's steely depths.

CHAPTER THIRTEEN

Far above the trees and the city, past a glamour that hid us from the Hums, Daniel and I flew down one of the rainbow roads that stretched like a net of iridescent ribbons across the city. I leaned forward and gripped the corners of the carpet, focusing my thoughts on home, but my mind kept wandering.

Ever since I'd been hit over the head with Imogen and Lucas, I'd been trying to stay busy. I'd focused on math tests, on Lily, on my garden, on ACT and SAT prep, on anything that would keep me from thinking about them and especially *her*.

But now, with Lily's legs taken care of and nothing to distract me besides the occasional pumpkin carriage or broomstick passing us, it was impossible to hide from my thoughts.

Lily was in love with Evan. I was making all her dreams come true. She was risking everything to follow her heart.

And what was I doing?

Sitting around, moping about something I'd lost because I'd been too much of a good friend to rush Lucas.

How could I be a good godmother to other people when I couldn't even handle myself?

We landed around the corner from the house. I tossed up an invisibility glamour that would throw my parents off for a few seconds if they saw me, then hid the carpet in the garage before we went in the front door.

Even the pain of obsessing over my former best friend and my craptastic love life wasn't enough to distract me entirely from the discomfort of being home. The strain settled around my shoulders the second I walked in the door.

My mom stood in the foyer, her wand out and pointed at the dim yellow chandelier above us.

"I'm glad you're back. We are going to eat together tonight," she said the moment we were inside. "As a *family.*"

She jabbed her wand in our direction to punctuate her words, and we both jumped to the side before a spell could fly out and hit us. You could never be too careful around an emotional faerie.

Daniel raised his hands and edged away from her toward the stairs.

"Okay," he said.

She whirled on him. "Don't even *think* you're in my good graces, mister."

Startled by the anger in her voice, I looked up at Daniel. He groaned and dropped his hands to his sides, where they dangled like a gorilla's.

"Seriously?" he said.

"We will talk later," she said. "After your father is home to be part of the discussion."

"Like he cares," Daniel muttered, and stalked up the stairs.

I waited until he was gone before turning to Mom, who was glaring at the chandelier like it had personally done her wrong.

"What's wrong?" I said.

She turned back to the light and pointed her wand at it. A silver trail of dust rose off the dangling crystals and streamed through the air like a piece of thread before collecting in a gray pile in the middle of the floor.

"Your brother has been skipping school," she said. "Apparently, he thinks running off to Devyn's house is a better use of his time than getting an education."

Her jaw tightened and her eyebrows went up. She was raring for an argument. I glanced at the stairs.

"I need you to go help with dinner," she said before I could escape. "Chicken's in the oven. I want a side of spinach and onions."

Chopping vegetables and hovering over a hot stove sounded a lot less dangerous than standing here right now. I went to the kitchen before she could say anything else.

My phone buzzed in my pocket while I was slicing onions, a small magic shield around my head to block the fumes.

The vibration startled me. My phone hadn't gone off much since Imogen and I had stopped speaking. That should have been enough of a clue, but I still felt a flush of surprise and anger when I saw her name on the screen.

Imogen: I'm really not in a good place right now. There's some stuff going on in my life and I know you're mad at me but I need you. Can we talk? Please?

I ignored it. The time for talking was before she'd gone behind my back. And the time for asking for moral support with Maia's stupid wedding, or whatever she was freaking out over now, was definitely not right after she'd made out with Lucas and then acted like it was *my* fault.

I'd never thought I'd let some guy get between us. More to the point, I'd never thought I'd care enough about a guy to let this become an issue. Imogen got the boys. That was just how it was.

But this time was different. If the Oracle was right—and the Oracle was always right—Imogen had taken Lucas from under my nose, before he'd even had the chance to choose for himself. He'd been interested in me. I'd felt that, and I'd never done anything about it because he'd had a girlfriend and I'd tried to not be a sucky person.

We could have turned into something. But Imogen couldn't let me have even one victory if it meant she might lose out.

I'd spent our entire friendship handing her the spotlight, consoling her through her dramas and listening to her talk about her dozens of boyfriends. And now, the one time in our entire friendship I'd actually had a shot at some excitement of my own, she'd swooped in and snatched the possibility away from me.

Imogen Dann did not deserve a response.

The front door opened and then slammed, and I felt my stomach sink a little.

Dad was home.

Imogen's dad was yet another thing about her life I envied. He was a sweetheart, full of bad jokes and boundless affection for all seven of his daughters. And he was just one more thing Imogen took for granted.

She had no idea how good she had it. Maybe that was what made it so impossible for her to think about other people.

"Dinner is at six," I heard Mom say.

He didn't reply, probably put off by the way her voice sounded like it was about to snap like a rubber band. I heard his footsteps go up the stairs. His bedroom door closed. Mom came into the kitchen and I busied myself with pulling spinach out of the fridge.

She sat down on the other side of the marble island with her elbows on the slick surface and watched me. After a few minutes, she ran her hands through her hair and then propped her chin on her fists with a sigh.

"I'm going on a quest," she announced.

I looked up from the bag of spinach and stared at her. She was waiting for my reaction, so I decided to hold off on giving one.

"No kidding," I said.

"I'm leaving this Saturday," she said. "The timing isn't great, but the timing is never going to be great, is it?"

I blinked. "I guess not," I said.

I scraped the garlic and onions into a pan to brown and turned back to her, my elbows on the counter across from hers.

"Um, why? What kind of quest?"

"I don't know yet," she said.

She twisted her favorite ring, an antique gold one with a piece of quartz carved to look like a rose. A faint warmth always seemed to radiate from it, and no wonder. The thing was loaded with more charms than should be allowed on one piece of jewelry.

"I've signed up with an agency that matches faeries to Glimmering royalty around the world," she said. "There's a good chance I'll be down in Argentina."

"Why?" I repeated.

She knocked her knuckles together with her hands curled into loose, restless fists. A strand of dark hair had escaped from her ponytail, and it brushed against her cheek.

"I need to work on my gifts," she said. "I've spent a long time being your father's arm candy and he doesn't seem to appreciate it, so I'm going to go spend some time on me."

I couldn't fault her line of thinking. This announcement was the very definition of left field, but now that she'd said it, I couldn't even pretend to be surprised.

It wasn't like she hadn't been dropping hints for months. She'd been full of offhand remarks about moving across the country, or renovating an old Glim mansion hidden up in northern Washington, or starting an after-school enrichment program for Glimmering kids. It was like she'd been trying on ideas in a desperate race to make one of them fit. Some kind of midlife crisis had been brewing, and I was strangely relieved to find out that all she'd ended up doing was getting a job.

"So, divination skills or what?" I said.

She was good at divination. She hadn't really practiced in years, but once in a while she'd see a vision in the steam from the kettle, and her knack for predicting the weather made the local newscast look like an embarrassment.

"Yes, actually," she said. She tilted her head like she was surprised.

It struck me that I never acted like I paid much attention to her. The truth was, I didn't. She was my mom. It rarely occurred to me to remember she was a person, too.

"Good for you," I said, and I meant it. "How long will you be gone?"

"Just a week," she said. "It sounds like I might get placed on a minor job. A queen down there is on bed rest with her second pregnancy and needs someone to find her grandmother's enchanted dagger. It's hidden in the wetlands. Sort of tedious but it won't take long, and it's a good chance to get my feet wet."

"Literally," I said.

Dad's footsteps sounded in the hallway. Mom fell silent. I went back to sautéing onions.

Dad was a nightmare at dinner. Mom must have told him about Daniel, because we'd barely sat down before he turned to him and said sharply, "The Portland Institute's faerie-craft course starts Saturday and I expect you to be there."

It wasn't a question or an invitation. Daniel was going to go in for the magical equivalent of ACT prep whether he liked it or not. My grades and work at Wishes Fulfilled had been

EMMA SAVANT

enough to convince Dad that I'd make it into his beloved Imperial College of Faeries without extra help, but Daniel had nothing going for him in the school or work departments.

"I'm not going to a prep course," Daniel said flatly.

Dad's jaw twitched. He had the granite jawline of a model and spent most of his time clenching it.

"I don't believe that decision is up to you," he said.

"Well, I don't believe I'm going to be there," Daniel said. "And I don't believe you're going to skip work just to make sure I show."

He picked up a piece of drippy dark spinach, then let it drop back onto his plate with a plop.

"What else are you going to do with your time?" Dad said. "Dress up and spout poetry for a living?"

The silence was tangible enough that I expected it to shatter if anyone made a noise. Finally, Daniel let out a shallow breath. He glared at me across the table, but I widened my eyes and shook my head.

"Olivia didn't tell me," Dad said, though the disgust in his voice made it clear it would have been better for me if I had. "Sometimes I think you both forget that I'm on the Council. I have eyes everywhere. I know what goes on in this city."

"Reginald," Mom said, in a soft warning voice.

"And you haven't done a damn thing about it," he said without looking at her. "Our son is making a fool of himself all around the city and you haven't even noticed."

"Give me a little credit," Mom said. I was surprised at the acidity in her tone. She hadn't been that terse with him in a while, though maybe that was because they hadn't been speaking. "Daniel wants to be a writer. I think that's a fine profession."

Dad barked a laugh. It was an ugly sound with no humor in it.

"A profession?" he said. "Living on welfare while he writes poetry in our basement for the rest of his life?"

"I guess you'd rather I sell my soul and become some shitty Glim corporate sellout," Daniel said.

Dinner lay forgotten on the table.

Dad leaned forward, anger crackling around him like a warning. "You watch your mouth," he said.

"Everyone knows the Council's just there to look busy while the queen tries to solve all your problems," Daniel said. "Haven't caught the guy baiting the Hums yet, have you? I thought you had eyes everywhere."

Dad gripped the table. His knuckles turned white with the pressure.

"That Council has given you every goddamned opportunity you've ever had," Dad said. "All of which you've wasted."

I was looking around for an exit when Mom decided to just lob a grenade into the conversation and let it all go to hell.

"And Olivia's not attending the Imperial College," she said. "She's going to Oregon State University to study biology."

My phone buzzed.

I felt everyone's attention on me. My dad stared like he was trying to shoot laser beams out his eyes and burn a hole through my forehead. I wasn't entirely sure he couldn't do it.

"I need to take this," I said, gripping the phone in my hand so hard I could feel my heartbeat in my palm. "Might be work."

I bolted from the room before they could stop me.

I ran from the house and into the sultry evening air, my heart pounding. I was halfway around the block before I even looked at the phone. It was a text.

Lucas: Sorry to pry… What's going on with you and Imogen?

My stomach curdled into lumpy knots. Why couldn't it have been a stupid promo text from the world fusion pizza place a few blocks over letting me know about their weekly special? Or even Lorinda letting me know she'd decided to drop another hot mess of a case in my lap? Why did it have to be Lucas, and why did he have to mention *her?*

After typing and erasing the message four times, I finally sent back, *She'll tell you if she wants you to know.*

It was only a few moments before my phone buzzed again. I ignored it for a while in favor of staring at a calico cat sitting on the rock wall surrounding someone's front-yard-turned-vegetable-garden. The cat was always somewhere in the neighborhood. I had no idea whom it had originally belonged to. It blinked at me with lazy eyes and then sat down and started grooming itself with its back paw flexed high into the air like a ballerina's.

Finally, when I couldn't stand it a second longer, I turned the screen back on.

Lucas: She won't tell me, but she misses you and she's stressed about her sister's wedding. Anything I can do to help?

I was too tired to even laugh.

Olivia: Too late. Imogen knows what she did. She was way out of line. I have too much respect for myself to be friends with someone who treats me like that.

I had too much respect for myself, even if I wanted nothing more than to grab her away from whatever she was doing right now and have a panic attack over my parents and my client and even Lucas.

I'd been too distracted to realize the wedding was coming up. It would be here in a couple of weekends, and I'd promised her I'd be there.

But all bets were off. If we weren't going to be friends, I wasn't going to feel obligated to sit through another minute of her angst about her dress or her hair or her sister's seventy-third consecutive emotional breakdown.

Especially not when I couldn't trust that she was telling me the truth about any of it.

Especially not when I was about to have a breakdown of my own.

Before I could think it through, I pulled my phone up again.

Olivia: She knew I liked you. Friends don't stab each other in the back over guys.

I pressed Send. Immediately, I wished I could take it back. I was so stupid. And I was too crappy of a faerie to know any spells that could stop a text in midair.

I shoved the phone back in my pocket and kept walking, trying to ignore the possibility of it buzzing again and unable to think about anything else. But Lucas didn't reply.

CHAPTER FOURTEEN

"Did you do anything fun this weekend?" I said.

Madison, whom I had spoken to maybe twice so far this year, squeezed lotion on her hands. She massaged it in, sliding the ginger-scented goop in between her fingers and into her cuticles. She held out the bottle to me, but I shook my head.

"It was okay," she said. "I took my little sister to see a movie."

"How fun," I said. "Which movie?"

I forced myself to pay attention while Madison told me about the latest animated feature starring a bunch of talking animals. I looked at her to be polite, then realized she was looking intently at me while she spoke. So I kept looking intently at her. Every blink felt like a huge, meaningful gesture. Her eyes bored into mine.

I had forgotten how eye contact worked.

Making conversation with anyone who wasn't Imogen was impossible. Elle was great, but she was busy with Pumpkin Spice and Kyle. And I didn't have a lot of other friends.

All friendships are awkward at the beginning, I told myself.

But that wasn't true. Imogen and I had clicked in half a second.

Forcing friendships made them awkward at the beginning. But what else was I supposed to do? Sit around and wait for another Imogen to walk into my life? Or another Lucas?

I kept staring at Madison and listening to her talk about some celebrity who did the voice of a llama and got it "totally right, it was hysterical."

I wondered whether Lily even knew llamas existed. There was so much I had to teach her about the Humdrum world before she transformed in a week. She wouldn't know about Hum money, or transportation, or social norms, or anything else that would let her survive here.

And she didn't have to just survive. She had to pass as a normal-enough Hum that Evan could fall in love with her.

Not that I wanted Evan to fall in love with her.

When I was honest with myself, I wanted Evan to stick with his fiancée and for my twitterpated client to go back to the sea where she belonged. But the Oracle had ruled that one out, so it wasn't going to be that easy. Things never were.

I'd succeeded in Elle's case because I'd done the right thing. But this time? I didn't even know what the right thing was. Maybe it *was* Lily's destiny to break up Evan's relationship and become his wife. Maybe Evan and the fiancée, Isabelle, would have been miserable together. It was impossible to know without meeting them.

It was impossible to know even if I *did* meet them.

This whole case was nothing but shots in the dark, augmented by King Pacifica sending Lorinda angry messages every few days.

Madison was staring at me, waiting for an answer to a question I'd missed.

"What was that?" I said. "Sorry, I got distracted by Mr. Henricks coming in."

Our teacher had just entered the room, though he didn't seem ready to start class. He was one of only two Glim teachers in the entire school. Beyond my glasses, I saw the dark bronze swirls of sorcery around him.

"I said, have you been to the new dine-in theater downtown?" she said.

"No," I said. "I hadn't even heard of it. What is it?"

"It's a movie theater, but they have a bunch of tables and you can actually order dinner before the movie starts and they'll bring it to you while the movie's playing. Their Mediterranean pizza is to die for. We had a girls' night out there the other day and it was so amazing."

"That's awesome," I said. "I'll have to check it out."

And then, finally, Mr. Henricks was trying to get our attention and I was able to escape. Small talk was the actual worst, even when I was the one initiating it.

I hated Imogen, but in the privacy of my own head, I had to admit that school had gone by faster when she was around.

I halfway listened as Mr. Henricks talked on and on about *The Grapes of Wrath,* which we'd read over the summer. It had been a good book, but I wasn't in the mood to focus. Instead, I doodled in the corner of my notebook, tracing pictures of maple leaves and dahlias that looked like chubby fireworks.

I didn't even notice when the bell rang until people started to stand up around me and the sound of books and papers being shuffled around filled the air. Startled, I looked up, trying to act like I had been paying attention. But it didn't matter—Mr. Henricks would never call me on it. He was one of those Glims who stood in awe of my dad and the rest of the Council. As far as he was concerned, I was a stellar student.

A cluster of girls stopped in the aisle to talk, blocking my way out. It wasn't worth trying to get past them, so I sank back into my seat and kept doodling.

The other Glim teacher, Ms. Darlington, came into the room against the trickle of students. She was tall, with a large beaked nose. I'd had her for government last year and had a vague idea that she coached softball.

"Can you still do lunch?" she asked Mr. Henricks. "Sophie's coming but Bart got held up."

"Yeah, I'm coming," he said. "I'm glad I caught you alone, though. Have something interesting to tell you."

"Yeah?"

He glanced up at the students like he was worried one of them might overhear. But the cluster of girls ignored them as one of them started squealing about someone's concert tickets.

I tugged on my ear, and the noise in the room turned to a roar. I focused hard on the group in the aisle and tugged again. Their chatter slowly faded until I could hear Mr. Henricks' low voice clearly.

"The lights that have been going out at the park by my house?" he said. "They did it again last night."

She rolled her eyes, like she'd been expecting something interesting.

He glanced up at the students and wiggled his fingers. I glanced over my glasses and saw a shimmering gray shield go up, a common glamour that would filter their words to sound like boring conversation about the weather to any nearby Humdrums.

"Bart's still convinced it's an electrical failure but I guarantee there's something living there," Mr. Henricks said. "There

151

were traces of enchantments all over the place in the morning."

"Yeah, because Glim kids go there to hook up," Ms. Darlington said. "They've been doing that since I was in high school."

"Naw, I don't think so," Mr. Henricks said. "It doesn't feel like kid magic. My neighbor's been making jokes about ghosts."

"Ghosts, wow," Ms. Darlington said flatly. "So what is it, really?"

Before he had a chance to answer, she added, "That's what I thought. Come on, my next class starts in an hour."

I grabbed my books and slipped in behind the group of girls, who hadn't disbanded but were at least moving toward the door.

In the hall, I dropped my books off and leaned against my locker. Silently, I ran through the mental list of weird things I'd heard lately—aside from literally everything that came out of Lily's mouth, anyway.

In the last few months alone, Hums had moved out of two apartment buildings because they were "haunted," at least one person had been chased by snakes that had come out of a sewer and miraculously disappeared a few minutes later, four Humdrums had checked into the hospital with what looked like fairy bites, and an eccentric local politician had been overheard raving about how "those damn Wiccans" had "cursed" all the dogs in his neighborhood to bark in chorus every night for half an hour at a time. Now, something weird was happening at a park by Mr. Henricks' house.

Separately, those incidents weren't much to notice, let alone be concerned over. But together, they started to add up.

I'd noticed the occasional odd thing before Amani had gotten me involved, although that could have been the tiniest drop of my mom's divination-happy blood at work. Now, though, even Daniel knew about someone "baiting the Hums," and it was obvious the Council had gotten involved.

Stuff was definitely going on with my dad that he wasn't telling us about. Why else would my parents' marriage be so stressed?

The goal was fear, Amani had said. Well, whoever Eris was, they had it. They were scaring the Hums and they were scaring my dad.

I slammed my locker shut and started toward the cafeteria. My legs felt tight, like I had to walk harder and faster to escape my thoughts. I was moving so fast by the time I got to the end of the hall that I didn't even see anyone coming down the stairs until my shoulder slammed against someone else's.

I tensed and looked up, waiting for whoever it was to tell me off.

A second later, I found myself staring into Lucas' familiar eyes.

My entire body got hot, as if I'd just stepped into a sauna. My mouth opened and closed a couple of times, and then I stammered, "Sorry."

"Hey," he said, at exactly the same moment.

"Hey," I said, just as he added, "Oh, sorry."

Every swear word I knew paraded through my head in one long, hot stream. My hand flew to the back of my neck.

"Hi," I said. "Sorry. I didn't mean to, like, crash into you there. Just going to lunch."

"No need to apologize," he said.

He put one hand on the stair railing and leaned against it. Standing on the stair above me, he felt even taller than usual.

"The pizza's recognizable today," he said. "You probably should be running if you want to get there before everyone eats it all."

A choking sound pushed out of my throat. I guessed it was supposed to be a laugh.

How was I supposed to make Evan fall in love with Lily? I couldn't even have a conversation with someone I'd known since middle school.

A few strands of dark hair fall across Lucas' forehead as he leaned toward me.

"Can I ask you something?" he said. "While I've got you here? I mean, I haven't seen you a lot lately."

I pressed my tongue against the roof of my mouth to keep myself from speaking.

"Yes," I said, after I was sure nothing stupid was going to come out.

He looked past me for a second, then at his hand on the railing, then back at me.

"Are you planning on talking to Imogen?"

I felt my eyebrows go up and wished I could control my face. Like, at all.

"No," I said.

"Why not? She said you won't even look at her when you're in class together."

"She hasn't told you?" I said.

How had he not picked it up from my last text?

"Um," he said, searching my face. "No? Told me what?"

I blew a long puff of air out. The spot between my eyes felt tight as a wound-up spring. I rubbed it, bumping my glasses. I loved the way absolutely no magic appeared at their edges when I looked at him.

"It's nothing," I said. "It doesn't matter."

He opened his mouth, but I brushed past him.

"Better get to lunch before the pizza's gone," I said over my shoulder. "Good to see you."

It was a relief to be gone. I felt his eyes on me until I turned the corner on the landing of the stairs and disappeared from his view, but I didn't look back.

I'd gotten to the cafeteria later than everyone else, and the lunch line was long. We weren't technically allowed to have our phones out at lunch, but no one enforced that rule, so I pulled up a brainless game to play while I waited. Before the opening screen loaded, my phone buzzed.

Amani: Do you have time to talk?

Was it really a question? Pizza day or not, she was Queen Amani.

Olivia: Of course. Give me five.

Slipping out of the lunch line was easy. Find a place I wouldn't be disturbed was harder. Finally, I squeezed myself into the end stall of the upstairs bathroom no one ever used. All the other bathrooms in the building had been upgraded a couple of years ago, but this one still had cramped stalls covered with marker graffiti and a floor that looked like the grime between the chipped tiles could come to life at any second.

I pulled my wand out of my hair. I had to tug to get it free from my messy bun. It felt reluctant to come loose, and I didn't blame it. I'd barely used the thing in days. I pointed it at the door, visualizing a barrier that would keep out Hums. Keeping out everyone was a little beyond my skills, but there were so few Glims here it didn't matter.

Once inside one of the stalls, I locked the door and threw up another barrier, this one to muffle sound.

And then I pulled Queen Amani's silver ring out from under my shirt, where I'd been wearing it for months. Without taking it off its chain, I slipped it on my pinkie finger. The chain dug into my skin, not enough to be painful.

She was waiting. The tiny mirror shimmered to life.

"Are you alone?" she said.

Her face appeared tiny in the mirror, like I was looking through the wrong end of a pair of binoculars. Her hair seemed even wilder than usual.

"Yeah," I said. "We're safe."

"I imagine you don't have much time, so I'll come straight to the point," she said. "An underground newspaper just published an interview with someone who just moved out of Portland due to 'supernatural phenomena.' The article included a photo of what they called a ghost. I suspect it's a poltergeist that moved too fast for the camera to capture."

"People will think it's edited," I said. My thoughts flickered to Mr. Henricks' conversation. I opened my mouth to tell her about it, but she was already talking again.

"Hopefully," she said. "But that's not everything. A popular nightclub downtown shut down last night without warning. The owner disappeared. She's a Hum, but she was dating a

Glim a few months ago, so we're investigating. Might be related, might not, but I wanted you to hear about it from me."

Her words came faster and faster, gathering speed like a train.

"We had reports this morning of teenagers doing magic in the open downtown. I sent a team out to glamour the memories of passerby, but we won't be able to find them all. And we don't know who the teenagers are, because Eris is protecting them too well. This is the second time this has happened, and by the time my people get there, they're always gone. I need you to keep an eye on the teenagers, Olivia. Any Glims at your school. Stay focused on them. Let me know if you see anything strange."

"I don't really know any Glims at my school," I said.

"I know," she snapped. "I just… Just, let me know if you see anything weird, okay?"

She let out a long sigh and ran her fingertips back and forth across her forehead.

"I'm sorry," she said. "This is a lot to throw at you. I just need to know you're watching."

"I'm always watching," I said, and quickly, before she could say anything else, added, "I just heard from one of my teachers that there are traces of magic at the park by his house. His neighbors have been joking about ghosts but he thinks something's living there."

Even through the tiny mirror, I felt a twinge of the stress that zinged around her body like a rogue bit of electricity.

"Have you talked to the Oracle?" I said, as if the queen of the Glimmering world wouldn't have already thought about that. "Nothing goes on in this city she doesn't know about."

I thought about Imogen, and her cheating on her exam. If the Oracle could see that, surely she could see who was causing these problems.

Amani took a deep breath.

"We've talked," she said. "The Oracle and I collaborate pretty closely. She's watching, too. But she's…"

She blinked, hard, like she wanted to make everything disappear.

"Eris is something else," she said. "It's not something we've dealt with before. So I just need you to be on alert, okay?"

"Okay," I said.

Fear jolted and tingled down my spine. The Faerie Queen was terrified, and I was ready to promise her anything.

"I'll keep watching. I'll talk to people and see what I can learn."

"Okay," Amani said. I watched the lines between her eyebrows smooth out, though it seemed like it took a lot of effort. She rubbed her forehead again. "Okay. Thank you. I'll let you go. I just wanted to keep you in the loop."

"I appreciate it," I said, although I didn't, really. No one in our world wanted to see the Faerie Queen scared. The Faerie Queen didn't *get* scared. Or so I'd thought.

Amani's face rippled like a reflection in a pond and faded out.

I stared at my own fraction of a reflection in its surface for a moment, then whipped the ring off my finger and shoved it back under my shirt. It fell against my skin, tiny and light but somehow carrying more weight than it had a few minutes ago.

I closed the bathroom stall behind me and paused to check my reflection in the mirror. Expressiveness was a faerie trait, and my face betrayed me during moments like these. The anxiety shone clear in my high eyebrows and wide eyes.

I took slow, deep breaths, staring at myself in the mirror until I saw the intricate muscles beneath my skin begin to loosen and relax.

I reached for the door. It burst open for me. I jumped back, my heart pounding, but it wasn't Eris or anyone come to eavesdrop on my conversation with Amani.

It was Imogen. Her eyes were wide and her hair was pulled up into a tight ponytail.

For a brief second, I wanted to throw my arms around her. I hated how much I missed her stupid face. I tried to talk, but nothing would come out.

Then her face hardened.

"Didn't expect to find you here," she said.

The way she looked at me made my stomach flip over in pain. It wasn't just her expression, either. She looked all wrong. Her skin was pale and her eyes had dark circles under them that she hadn't bothered to cover up with a glamour or makeup, but it wasn't her appearance that unsettled me. It was her aura. She felt cold and harsh, and so menacing that my skin crawled with the need to escape.

Had she always been like this, and I'd just been too stupid to notice?

"It's a good place to be alone," I said. My voice came out sharper than I meant.

"That's why I use it," she said.

Her voice was so icy that I took a step back. She folded her arms and stared at me, her thin eyebrows high, like she was waiting for an apology or something.

"Also?" she said. "It would be cool if you could stop texting my boyfriend."

My skin flashed hot, and I knew in half a second that my face had betrayed me again.

No wonder Lucas hadn't mentioned my text. He'd probably forgotten all about it, thanks to one of her glamours.

Screw apologies. I threw the door open again and blew past her.

CHAPTER FIFTEEN

Evan's photography studio was in an old brick building in a shopping area nestled at the foot of a cliff in Oregon City. Large black-and-white photos of naked babies and colorful prints of families filled his studio windows. The words *Evan Costner Photography* hovered in the corners of the prints and ran along the window in black and gold vinyl letters.

A bell tinkled gently when I opened the door. I jumped and my hand twitched, ready to fly to my wand. I pressed the hand firmly against my hip.

It had been a week since I'd spoken to Queen Amani, and everything still made me jump. I hadn't heard about any more Humdrum attacks, but some crazy part of myself still thought every unexpected sound was Eris bursting into the room. I let out a long breath and let the door click closed behind me.

I was alone in the lobby. Two long photographs of water-falls framed a shadowed doorway that probably led to the portrait room. I looked around for a bell, but then I heard foot-steps. A moment later, Evan stepped out into the lobby.

He looked just like his photo, with sandy hair, hazel eyes, and a pleasant but uninteresting face. He looked down at me and smiled—a nice, vague smile that didn't tell me anything.

"Hi," I said. "Are you, um, the photographer?"

He held out a hand. I took it. His skin was warm and soft.

"I'm Evan," he said. "What can I help you with?"

Tell me if you're worth it, I thought. *Tell me if the Oracle is right in thinking I should help you destroy your life so you can marry a mermaid. Prove to me that granting Lily's wish isn't going to screw up everything and make me feel like crap for the rest of my life. Tell me I'm not helping Lily do to Isabelle what Imogen did to me.*

"I was just admiring your pictures," I said.

I waved vaguely toward the window. I'd meant to go in and pretend to be sort of clueless. Now that I was here, I realized I hadn't exactly needed to plan that.

"Thank you," he said. His smile warmed. "That's very nice of you to say."

"Is that the kind of photography you usually do?" I said. "Families and babies and stuff?"

I mentally kicked myself. I wanted to stop everything, go outside, rehearse an intelligent conversation, and then try this again. But if I couldn't handle this without tripping over my tongue, I definitely was not up to a time-rewind spell, even if they were legal.

"I do a little bit of everything," Evan said. He nodded at the waterfall on his right. "Are you interested in having some pictures taken?"

"Maybe," I said. "I'd never noticed you here before."

"I just moved to this location," he said.

He had nice eyebrows, I thought. Maybe Lily was into eyebrows. He seemed nice, but "nice" wasn't usually enough to inspire her kind of passion.

Then again, no one had ever accused mermaids of waiting around for passion to find them.

I shifted and adjusted my purse strap over my shoulder. What had I thought I was going to do? March in here and ask him if he still had the hots for his fiancée or if he'd be willing to abandon her for a lovesick mermaid, just theoretically speaking?

"Are you in high school?" he said.

"Yeah," I said.

He stepped behind a tall counter that stood in the corner. I heard a soft shuffling sound, and then he held out a business card with a picture of a maple leaf on the front.

"Keep me in mind for senior photos," he said.

He had so much pleasant hope in his voice I felt like some swell kid from the fifties was asking if maybe I'd consider being his girl.

I took the card from him and made a show of examining it before I put it in my purse.

"I'll give you all the shots in digital and a bunch of prints, just for the price of the prints," Evan said, and winked.

Okay, he was a little charming. But still.

There was nowhere to go from here. I offered a bright smile and said, "Thanks. Well, I guess I should probably go."

"You have a good day," he said, like he meant it.

I waved awkwardly as I moved toward the door. "You too."

He was nice. He also didn't seem like the kind of guy who'd cheat on his fiancée. I turned back, trying to find the words to ask him about her.

"Do you do weddings?" I blurted. "My friend's older sister is getting married soon and I think she's looking for a photographer."

Since I was totally welcome at *that* wedding.

"I don't," he said. "I can give her some recommendations, though, if she'd like to stop by."

"Oh," I said. "What about you? Are you married?"

He smiled, confused. "No," he said. "Not yet. I will be soon, though."

To the right girl, I urged silently.

"Congratulations," I said.

I couldn't think of anything else to say. I mentally kicked myself about fifty times and walked out.

My mom's errands were much easier. A new item had appeared on the shopping list since this morning, written in my mom's loopy handwriting: *Crystal pendulum (small ones underneath front counter, ask if you're not sure).* I'd gotten that first, and now I was trying to figure out which rune set she wanted.

I hadn't even known my mom could read runes, but here I was, trying to decide between the amethyst "Summer Wishes" and the black onyx "Midnight Dreams." Apparently, rune kits were named by the same people who marketed dollar-store candles and mall-kiosk perfume.

After my underwhelming meeting with Evan, it was a relief to be here and engaged in the relatively simple task of picking out divination supplies. Worst-case scenario with shopping was that Mom would have to return something when she got home next week. Compared with the other worst-case scenarios of an angry Sea King, an Eris so powerful he or she scared Queen Amani, and an Imogen who wasn't my friend anymore, the pressure of choosing the right runes felt like a trip to the Bahamas.

Mom had been wearing a lot of purple lately. I dropped the box of amethyst stones into my basket, and turned to the next item on the list: *Balsam fir essential oil.*

Amber bottles not much bigger than my thumb sat on a multi-tiered shelf on the other side of the cluttered shop. The woman behind the counter glanced up at me, then returned to browsing her magazine. I skimmed the labels. *Allspice, Angelica Root, Anise Seed,* and there it was, *Balsam Fir.* I dropped the glass bottle carefully into my basket before I looked over Mom's list for any oils I hadn't noticed earlier.

"You should try the jasmine," a voice said behind me. "The smell is heaven. Good for love spells, too, though I don't necessarily recommend that."

A glance over my shoulder confirmed that the voice did, in fact, belong to Queen Amani. She was keeping her energy locked down; I hadn't even felt her walk up.

"Hi," I said. "What are you doing here?"

"Same as you," she said. "Shopping. Wendy's good about leaving me alone."

It took me a second to realize Wendy must be the faerie behind the counter. Amani reached over my shoulder and selected a bottle of juniper oil.

"How have you been?"

I stared at her. Last time we'd spoken, she'd hardly been asking about my day.

"I've been fine," I said.

Her gold-threaded curls were as wild as ever, but her face had smoothed out.

"You seem… calmer," I said.

One of her fingers twitched. Beyond my glasses, the white bubble of a sound-blocking spell shimmered around us so thickly I could barely see the room around us. I knew how to throw up sound bubbles, but this was something else. With the tiniest movement, she'd managed to conjure something so strong I couldn't have matched it even with hours of preparation and focus.

And she'd thought I could be the next Faerie Queen.

"I am. I apologize," she said. "I wasn't in the best state of mind when I mirrored you. I should have waited until I was able to compose myself."

"It's fine that you called then," I said. "I was just a little worried. I've probably been assuming things are worse than they are."

"Oh, they're worse," she said.

She tucked a strand of hair behind her ear. One of her gold bracelets glistened in the yellow light of the shop.

"Things are worse than even I imagined," she said. "But I feel more prepared to deal with them than I did."

I glanced at her basket. In addition to the juniper oil, she carried four small packages of herbs, a box of white candles, a single braid of mermaid hair, a grapefruit-sized crystal ball with intricate symbols etched in a circle around its top, and a crystal bottle of sprite tears.

It had never occurred to me that Queen Amani might do her own shopping, let alone for basic magic supplies.

"I'm glad you're feeling better about it," I said. "I'm sorry. I wish I could do more to help."

"You still might," she said. "I haven't been asking you to keep an eye out for nothing, you know."

"Telling you things isn't the same as helping," I said. I might get lucky enough to overhear a clue as to who Eris was. But I didn't expect to stumble on the truth.

I looked over my glasses at the silence bubble. It shimmered strong and white.

"Even if you figure out who the person is, what are you going to do about it?" I said. "If they're managing to hide from even you and the Oracle, they're probably pretty powerful."

"They're definitely powerful," Amani said. "I've decided to cross that bridge when I come to it."

She smiled at me, and she really did seem fine. The knot that had lived in my stomach since we last spoke loosened a little. "That sounds smart," I said.

"So what are you doing here?" Amani said, nodding toward my basket. "You didn't strike me as the rune-reading type."

"They're for my mom," I said. "She's been working on her divination lately and needed some supplies for spells. She's in Argentina and wanted me to pick all this stuff up before her plane gets in. I just got off work and, you know, beats going home."

I pressed my lips together. *Stop babbling,* I silently ordered.

Amani opened her mouth as if she were going to ask a question, then closed it again and reached for a polished black river stone from a box on one of the shelves next to us.

"So you're not into divination?"

"I'm not into magic," I said.

Amani already knew that. She turned the smooth stone over in her hand.

"Would you mind trying something for me?"

I tried to scan her energy, but she was locked down tight and I couldn't pick anything up.

"Sure," I said. It came out as a question.

She handed me the stone. "Look at that and tell me what you see."

The surface was black, smooth, and unremarkable.

"A stone," I said. But that was a stupid answer. "It's smooth," I said. "And it's not quite a perfect oval. It's pretty thin. Would probably be a good skipping rock."

"Soften your eyes and look again," she said. "But this time, try to see inside the stone."

I looked up sharply.

"I told you, I'm not into divination."

"I know," she said. "It probably won't come to anything. Humor me."

I tried to soften my gaze the way I'd always heard you should. The stone seemed to blur a little bit, and I tried to look deep inside it. Beyond it, the cloudy white of the soundproof bubble floated like a blank screen.

Amani stayed silent, waiting. After a moment, I started to see the way the light played on the stone's edges, and noticed how many tiny pores covered its otherwise smooth surface. And then, very faintly, I saw something move.

It was impossible to tell if it was just my eyes playing tricks, protesting staring so hard. A tiny flutter appeared, flickers of yellow lamplight in a vague pattern.

"I think it's a flower," I said. "A rose, maybe?"

Talking broke my focus. The hazy impression disappeared immediately, leaving only a rock in my hand.

Amani sighed. I handed the stone back to her. It was a relief to feel its weight leave my palm. I watched as she set it back on the shelf.

I was the worst faerie in the world.

I wished the shop would just swallow me up right there and let me disappear into its cluttered aisles.

My phone beeped from inside my pocket.

"I'm sorry," I said.

"Oh, no worries," Amani said. She waved an airy hand, as if it were possible to just brush off my mediocrity. "This isn't the easiest environment to concentrate in."

"Also I suck at divination," I said.

"Everyone sucks at divination," she said. "People who are good at it just suck marginally less."

Her graciousness was another quality of a good Faerie Queen I did not have. The only comforting thought was that Imogen didn't share that particular quality, either. I bit back the sudden urge to ask Amani if she'd given any thought to my stupid idea of considering my former best friend as her heir.

Amani took a deep breath, like she wanted to sigh but was being too tactful. Suddenly, all I wanted was to finish Mom's shopping so I could go home and be alone in my room with my plants.

"I'm sorry," she said.

I looked up. She frowned at me with her eyebrows drawn together.

"You must be so sick of running into me all the time," she said. "If I were better at this I'd leave you alone."

"Better at what?"

She shrugged, holding up both her hands like she was lifting invisible weights.

"Life," she said. "I keep seeing you in my divinations and I know there has to be a reason for it."

"Maybe you just suck at divination," I said.

It was supposed to be a joke, but the second the words were out of my mouth I wanted to die. I waited for the ground to swallow me up, or for the Faerie's Queen's rage to knock me down with a bolt of lightning.

Instead, Amani cracked up.

"There is so much more truth to that than I want to admit to," she said.

My phone beeped again.

"You can get that if you need to," Amani said. "I should probably get on with my shopping anyway."

"That's okay," I said, but then I reached into my pocket anyway, just to make sure it wasn't Mom.

Amani gave me a tiny wave and walked down the row to examine a drawer filled with tiny pink and purple crystals. The white bubble around us thinned and dissolved, like clouds blowing away in a breeze. The colors of the shop seemed too rich without it.

Imogen: Hey. I need to talk to you.

Imogen: Stop ignoring me. You're being kind of an ass. This is important.

I glared at the phone so hard the screen shut off without my having to press the button.

Amani made a sudden, jerky movement in the corner of my eye. "Whoa," she said.

I looked up and saw her staring at me with furrowed eyebrows.

"You okay?"

"I'm fine," I said. I shoved the phone back in my pocket.

"You sure?" she said.

I gritted my teeth. "Yes," I said. "It's just an… acquaintance. The girl I told you about when we were in the Garden, actually."

I stepped toward her and lowered my voice. Even though the shopkeeper was Amani's friend, I didn't want our connection getting around.

"I told you I thought she might be a good candidate for your heir," I said, keeping my voice on a tight leash. "I was mistaken."

"That's too bad," Amani said. The phrase was a question, one I was more than willing to answer.

"She's not reliable," I said. "Turns out she's massively dishonest, actually. Not a great choice for a queen."

"Sounds like not," Amani said. "Tact is sometimes required but dishonesty isn't ideal. Wasn't she one of your best friends?"

"Best friend," I said. "Because I have horrible taste in people."

"Yeah, me too, sometimes," Amani said.

That, I seriously doubted. But the attempt at empathy was kind of her. It felt nice to have someone try to be kind.

"So, just so you know," I said.

"Thanks."

She turned back to browsing. Her eyes were suddenly far away, so far I didn't think I'd reach her if I spoke again.

CHAPTER SIXTEEN

"Your world is so loud!" Lily said.

She stumbled to the window and slid the old frame shut, blocking out the noise of traffic roaring behind her. She wobbled on her legs, tottering every few steps like she would go down any moment, and held onto the wall as she inched back to sit on her bed beside me.

A blue-haired muse ducked her head into the room, looked around, checked something on her clipboard, and disappeared back out through the open doorway.

We were at the Mother Gemma J. Goose Halfway House for Transitioning Archetypes. The old building buzzed with magic; at the edge of my glasses, I could see sparks, pink clouds, and swirling glitter tornados revolving through the place. Pulsing music streamed in from another room, its steady beat and Arabian melody making me think a crazy genie party was about to start. Every few seconds, loud conversation or laughter floated through the door and the walls.

"This building isn't representative," I said.

"That's a good point," Lily said. "I have to remember, nothing is representative. I didn't realize how far technology had progressed here! It's one thing to watch the cars on the highway but it's quite another to see them right outside your window. Our machines don't change so often below."

"I don't imagine there's a lot of Humdrum influence," I said.

"Hardly any," she said. "And I hadn't realized how many Humdrums there are here! I have no idea how you all camouflage yourselves."

"You'd better learn quick," I said.

But I wasn't worried. The Halfway House was designed for oddballs like Lily, Heroes and Heroines and Sidekicks stuck between worlds. The community bulletin board outside advertised classes with titles like *Hop to It!: Integrating Your Inner Amphibian After an Extended Transformation* and *Tree Huggers: Connecting with Nature in the Concrete Jungle (fall session for faeries, dryads, and naiads only).*

Lorinda had slipped me a flyer about this place a few days before Lily had sprinkled her potion and come to land. She didn't say a thing, but it seemed like the Oracle had talked to her—and it was a good thing, too, because I'd been driving myself crazy trying to figure out how I'd be able to book Lily a hotel room without getting in major trouble with the Wishes Fulfilled budget office.

Goose House was better than a hotel. Lily could be herself here until she learned to pass for human.

"I stopped by Evan's work a couple days ago," I said.

Lily's eyes brightened.

"Where is it? I know how to find him from the river. But I don't know how to get to Oregon City from here."

"Good," I muttered.

"What did he say?"

She swept her hair up into a ponytail with her hand, then let it fall loose again around her shoulders.

The transformation had taken everything mermaid about her and turned it human. The strands of seaweed woven through her auburn hair had melted into vivid green-dyed streaks that shifted through the red. The seashells and sea glass were still there, woven into the tiny braids and dreadlocks that fell at random past her shoulders. Her style was unusual enough to turn heads anywhere but Portland, and she had retained every bit of her fierce mermaid beauty.

Evan would be an idiot if he didn't at least look twice when he saw her next.

"He seems… nice," I said.

I fished the business card out of my purse and handed it to her. She stared at it for a moment like she was trying to absorb the paper through her eyeballs, then clutched it to her chest.

Giving her the summary of our conversation took all of thirty seconds. It wasn't much, but she gazed at me in rapt attention as though memorizing every word that fell from my lips.

"I love him," she said fervently.

It wasn't the first I'd heard of this, but I still couldn't imagine not being confused by it.

"How do you know that?" I said. "Like, really? I get that the Oracle agrees with you and everything, but how do you know? You've talked to him, what, twice?"

"Three times," she said. "I don't need more."

Did I love Lucas? If I couldn't tell, did that mean it wasn't love?

Not that it mattered.

"You have to need more than that," I said. "You can't build a whole relationship on three meetings and you *definitely* can't give up your entire life for it. Aren't you supposed to be really into art or something?"

I waved my hand at her legs, which sat neatly folded together under a short ruffled skirt.

"Yes, I can," she said. "And Evan *inspires* my art."

The sincerity in her voice threw me off. She leaned forward, her fists pressing into the pink coverlet on either side of her and her legs swinging against the mattress' edge. Her toes stuttered against the floor when her teal ballet flats hit the wooden floorboards.

"Just because I'm crazy for doing this doesn't mean I shouldn't."

She did realize she was crazy, then.

I put my elbow up on the back of my chair and leaned my head against my hand, watching her.

"What's your logic?" I said. A second later, it occurred to me that logic was probably not the thing Lily used to guide her decisions.

"I know everyone thinks I'm out of my mind," Lily said. "Everyone always thinks the Little Mermaid Archetypes are out of our minds. Why give up everything for some guy I don't know, right?"

I shrugged. "You said it first," I said.

"I know things might not work out with Evan," she said.

I sat up straight.

"Then why are you here? This is kind of a big deal. I don't know if your dad is even going to let you back into the ocean again if things don't work out."

I'd received a strongly worded message from him the day Lily had transformed. A dove had dropped a fist-sized seashell onto my desk and King Pacifica's voice had bellowed out of it, blustering about bad decisions and professional responsibility and his lawyers. Lorinda had taken the shell from me with tight lips and said she'd "deal with it." I wasn't sure what that meant, but I *was* sure we were on his bad side.

"So what?" she said. "Even if everything goes wrong, at least I tried." She looked out the window for a moment, then back at me, her delicate face fierce with passion. "I don't want to live with regrets. We only get one life and I want to *live* mine. You always regret the things you *don't* do more than the things you *do* do. Always."

It was human and faerie nature both to make everything in the world about me. My thoughts turned inward almost immediately.

What did I regret?

I regretted not going after Lucas when I had the chance. I regretted not spending more time with him, and with other friends who weren't Imogen.

At the same time, I regretted getting so angry with Imogen that I felt like I couldn't reach out to her even if I wanted to.

I regretted not standing up to my dad and telling him my college plans before my mom got to it, especially since she'd been off in Argentina and I'd been stuck at home navigating his icy silent treatment.

And if I was honest and let myself tell the truth for one brief moment, I almost—almost—regretted telling the Faerie Queen I didn't want to follow in her footsteps.

That wasn't a real one. Of course I didn't want that kind of responsibility, or to be locked into the Glimmering world forever. But wouldn't I always wonder *what if?*

Lily was wrong about a lot of things, but maybe she was right about this. If I had anything to regret, it was my lifetime of being a doormat. It was all the times I hadn't made strong decisions, and all the times I'd hidden and pretended I didn't care about who I was and what I wanted, and all the times I'd said "no" because "no" sounded safer than "yes."

Had I ever been strong about who I was? That kind of thing took courage. I hadn't even been brave enough to tell Imogen straight to her face that she'd hurt me.

Imogen was my best friend. She was supposed to be the safest person in the world, and instead of talking, I'd just shut her out. If I couldn't even force myself to have a civil conversation with her, what did that say about me?

Lily was right: All my regrets were built around fear. But I knew fear best.

A chime rang in the hall, and a voice called out, "Lunchtime!" Lily didn't move. She was too busy staring at me like she was trying to download her brain to mine through her gaze.

"The only thing that matters in this life is relationships," she said, and she sounded like she knew that more solidly than I knew my own name. "People and your love for them are more important than anything. You've got to be willing to put your heart on the line for the people that matter." She took a deep breath. "And that's what I'm doing. I'm putting my heart on the line, because I think Evan matters."

I was busy trying to figure out who and what mattered to me when Lily spoke again. "And maybe it'll kill me," she said, her voice soft but resolute. "But at least I won't spend my whole life wondering what had happened if I'd taken a chance. That's better, isn't it?"

CHAPTER SEVENTEEN

I couldn't get Lily's voice out of my head. I'd spent all night listening to her over and over: *People and your love for them are more important than anything. You've got to be willing to put your heart on the line for the people that matter.*

Imogen mattered.

That didn't mean I wasn't angry with her. Thinking about what she'd done still made me fiery inside. She was self-centered, and she'd hid the truth from me to get something we both wanted. But we'd been best friends for too long for me to let her go over some guy.

She knew it, if her texting me every few weeks meant anything. And I knew it now, too. I had to at least give her a chance to explain herself.

I poked a pair of rhinestone earrings through my ears and glanced in the mirror to give my hair a last once-over. Imogen had better realize how serious I was to not only show up at her sister's wedding, but also wear makeup and honest-to-god hair product on top of it.

I'd made the short trek to Imogen's house a thousand times growing up. It had never made me nervous before now.

And of course, I was alone. Mom had gotten back from her Quest late last night and had slept through most of the day, waking only to ask me to apologize to the Danns and let them know she was feeling under the weather. Dad was at work, and he hadn't sent his apologies, probably assuming Mom would cover for him like always. And Daniel was stuck at his magical prep course, just like Dad had threatened.

After months of searching for the right space, Maia had decided to get married in their family's backyard, which had been the first place anyone had suggested to her. The day had—probably with some magical help—turned out to be sunny and clear. Cars lined the streets and a motley array of broomsticks, flying carpets, and cut crystal jars of bubbles cluttered the porch behind a Humdrum glamour. Another Humdrum glamour arced over the property; if I looked over my glasses, I could see the dome shimmering over the house like a bubble.

I stepped under an archway covered in climbing roses and into the backyard, where dozens of colorful birds sat tamely on the hedges and eaves, piping songs to one another. The yard pulsed with faeries and witches and magicians all throwing their arms around each other and catching up on the latest gossip.

The Dann family's Glimmering gatherings were the loudest celebrations I had ever attended. Imogen's old-blood family line was as big a deal as mine, but her parents were nice, and they used their social clout mostly to throw fabulous parties. Their gatherings were about affection and laughter instead of stiff political angling.

The only bad part was getting past the dozens of acquaintances waving for my attention. I smiled and ducked under the arm of a witch reaching out for me. The cobwebby fabric of her sleeve brushed soft against my face. She looked vaguely familiar.

"Sorry," I called over my shoulder. "Have to find someone."

I scanned the crowd and finally spotted Imogen up front, standing in her sickly yellow bridesmaid dress next to a cluster of her sisters. They were all tall and willowy with fabulous hair. Imogen looked like a gawky little kid next to them, and given Imogen's uncomfortably good looks, that was saying something.

Despite the dress, she looked better than the last time I'd run into her. The bags under her eyes were gone and her skin had a healthy glow. I felt an unexpected relief at the sight.

She wasn't the only person here I recognized. Elle and Kyle stood not too far away from her, talking only to each other like they felt out of place. I waved at Elle, and she smiled and started edging toward me before Imogen's mom caught her. Mrs. Dann was a master mingler and wanted to know everything about everyone.

Before I could catch Imogen's eye, Mr. Dann stood up and clapped his hands for attention. Each clap sounded louder than the last, and by the time he spoke, his voice boomed as if through a loudspeaker.

"If everyone could take a seat," he said. "We'll be starting in just a few minutes."

The chairs on the lawn were formed out of vines that grew up from the ground and twisted together to form swirly green wicker seats. Gold cushions had been placed on them for comfort. I sat halfway to the front as a quartet of violinists and a harpist began playing. Conversations around me rose and fell against the music.

I watched Imogen as she walked past the crowd and behind a grape arbor, where other members of the wedding party seemed to be gathering behind the thick green leaves.

Ten minutes later, the procession started. As was customary at Glim weddings, the guests sent sparks and fairy dust in arcs over the aisle, showering the bridesmaids and groomsmen with light and making the event look like the inside of a firework. I flicked my wand over Imogen when she passed on the arm of an awkward-looking college guy, hoping she would somehow feel it and know my purple glitter was a tiny peace offering.

The groom, Andrew, was tall and skinny, with knees and elbows that seemed to take up too much of his attention. He wore rectangular wire glasses and bounced on the balls of his toes. He looked like a dork—a nice one.

Then the music changed to a sweeping march, and Maia came down the aisle. She was radiant, but my attention rapidly switched from her face to her gown. Thousands of downy white feathers trailed down from her hip and splashed across the skirt, foaming around her ankles like a pillow had exploded. I could only imagine Imogen's face when she'd seen it. But Imogen had figured out how to control her expression between then and now, and she watched Maia with a vacant, pleasant face that revealed nothing going on in her head.

The ornithologist groom clasped his hands together as though trying to keep them from flying away. His bouncing increased as Maia approached, making him look like a kid who was about to be handed a lollipop.

It was hard to keep from liking a guy who could get that excited over Maia in a terrifying bird dress.

And then they said a bunch of corny things to each other, and the faerie who married them pronounced them man and wife. They kissed and the backyard exploded into cheers.

Sparkles and golden ribbons shot out of people's fingers and wands, a dozen brightly plumed parrots were released from a magician's top hat and promptly fled, squawking, to hide in one of the trees, and I ducked to avoid a pointed witch's hat that had been thrown in celebration and come down on the wrong side of the aisle.

Wedding melded into reception in a matter of minutes. With a whisk of Mr. Dann's hand, the chairs swiveled to face the empty expanse of the lawn, their vines creaking. Mrs. Dann and one of Imogen's sisters both pointed their wands out toward the lawn. The grass bent down as though in a heavy wind, and thousands of tiny blades wove together and stiffened into a springy green dance floor. Lights twinkled on in the trees circling the lawn and the violinists and harpist started up with livelier music.

"I love this song!" a woman behind me shrieked, and she dragged two of her friends onto the dance floor with her.

In moments, it was full of people moving their bodies in every way imaginable. Some wiggled their butts and waved their arms like they were at a nightclub, others leapt into waltzes and foxtrots that didn't quite match the music, and one faerie in the corner seemed to be performing a one-woman ballet.

Despite the differences, they were united in being happy that one more set of young lovers had found each other. For a moment, my heart flushed with the glow of my community. I forgot it most of the time, but these were my people every bit as much as my dad's self-important friends were. This kind of raucous celebration was just as Glim as prestigious magic schools and godmothering jobs. I didn't get to see it much, but there was another side to my world—and it was pretty darn okay.

I caught a glimpse of Imogen on the other side of the dance floor. One of her sisters, Nicole, was talking to her. Imogen's arms were folded and her mouth was pressed into a thin line. I had a feeling Nicole was being pressuring her to dance or do photos.

I hadn't been there for her through any of this. The guilt in my stomach felt like a living thing.

I had taken two steps toward her when I caught a conversation between two women still sitting on the vine chairs.

"She thinks it's haunted," one said. Her hair was swept up into a silver beehive, and it wobbled as she nodded toward the other woman.

As happened every time I heard that word, *haunted,* my thoughts flickered to the silver ring hidden under my clothes.

"Humdrums do seem fond of that idea."

The other woman, about the same age but with a dark, spiked pixie cut, didn't seem impressed. She tugged on one of her enormous dangling red earrings.

"I had a woman in my neighborhood saying the same thing," she said. "Electrical failure? It's haunted. Can't find their keys? Haunted. I swear, for not believing in our world, they seem obsessed with magic."

"This one's different," the silver-haired woman said. "She had me come over, and there was something strange going on in that house. Something strange, I'm telling you. I couldn't narrow it down. Normally I can find the source of a spell, as you well know. Could have gotten rid of the problem for her. But this one I just couldn't track."

"She knows you're Glim?"

"No, nothing like that." She waved a dismissive hand. "Just a younger woman in the neighborhood, comes to me with her parenting questions. She has two kids under seven and all mine turned out to manage adulthood well enough, so she likes my advice."

She patted the back of her hair.

I held my breath to hear more of the conversation, but they'd moved on. The red-earring woman started talking about her youngest granddaughter's first birthday and how she only wanted to eat the frosting flowers on her cake after Grandma enchanted them to sparkle.

I wanted to sit and wait for the conversation to circle back around, or to just point-blank ask them for more, but I couldn't. Imogen had detached herself from her sister and stood alone.

I sent a tiny pulse of energy toward her, hoping to catch her attention before someone else did. She looked up sharply, and then her eyes met mine. I waited for a smile, or at least a look that said she didn't want me to leave. But her face stayed blank, and her eyes stayed cool.

I waited until I was close enough to talk without shouting.

"Hey," I said.

"You came." Her words were clipped and distant. Around her, over the edges of my glasses, a strange pale pearly glamour shimmered. Her glamours had never felt or looked like that before. She'd probably thrown herself into her Glim studies after we'd stopped talking and learned all kinds of new enchantments.

I bit the inside of my cheek. "I'm sorry I haven't been around," I said.

"It's fine."

She looked away, scanning the crowd like I wasn't even there.

"Obviously not."

Not thirty seconds into the conversation, and my tone had gotten dry and sarcastic. I tried again, keeping it carefully casual, like I didn't really care about the answer and supported her no matter what decisions she made.

"Is Lucas here?"

She snorted, or whatever the elegant, composed version of a snort was.

"He's a Humdrum, Olivia," she said, like I was a toddler. "Clearly he wasn't invited."

"Oh," I said. "Right. Well… I just meant, it was okay if he was."

"Of course it would be okay if he was," she said, each word slow and clear. "He's my boyfriend. Why wouldn't it be okay for him to be at my sister's wedding?"

Everything I said just crammed my foot further into my mouth. I pinched my lips shut, then let out a sigh, hoping my muscles would take the hint and relax.

"Look," I said. "I know you're mad at me and I'm sorry. Can we talk?"

"Not the best time," Imogen said. "Kind of in the middle of something."

She wouldn't look at me. She just kept scrolling her eyes past the crowd behind my head, waiting for anything more interesting to get her away from the tedium of my company.

I sucked on the inside of my cheek. I had to stay calm.

"I'm sorry," I said. "I came to support you. How about tomorrow?"

"Not a good time either," Imogen said. "Actually, you know what? There is no good time. Like, ever."

With no warning, my eyes started to prickle. I blinked the sensation back down.

"What's wrong with you?" I said, and again my voice was sharper than I meant. "I'm trying to apologize."

Imogen snapped her gaze to me. The force of the anger blazing in her eyes made me step back.

"I know he's been texting you," she said. "He's been weird around me for days, and then I saw your name on his phone. Your name, Olivia."

A dozen responses flew into my head, all reminding her that she had been dishonest with me first. And then they were followed by puzzlement, because actually, Lucas hadn't been texting me. Unless she meant—

"You're not talking about the other week?" I said. "Imogen, that was about *you*. Lucas is worried about you because you've been all weird, and he thinks you and I need to fix this broken, crappy thing we used to call a friendship. I happen to agree."

She laughed. The sound made the hairs on my arms prickle like she'd just run her fingernails over a chalkboard.

"Like I want to be friends with you," she said.

People around us were starting to look. Her voice was rising, and I wanted to grab her and make her quiet down, but didn't dare. Her fingers twitched at her sides and yellow sparks shot from them.

"As if I want to spend all my time dealing with your neuroses and trying to coach you into not being terrified of scary *boys* and listening to you whine about biology school and your parent's shitty marriage falling apart!"

The last words ended on a yell. The lawn around us fell silent. A woman paused with a glass of red wine halfway to her lips. I saw Mrs. Dann put a silent hand over her mouth before grabbing one of Imogen's sisters and pushing her towards us.

I couldn't move. Imogen's face began to blur as hot tears rushed to my eyes and made the whole world look like it was swimming. My mouth opened and closed a few times, but nothing came out.

I hadn't even made her promise not to tell anyone that. I'd trusted her. Even when we weren't talking, I'd been stupid enough to assume I wouldn't need to ask her not to tell.

"I hate you," I whispered. It was the only thing I knew.

My hands clenched at my sides, but still I couldn't move.

And then a gentle hand was on my arm, and someone's voice in my ear said, "Come on, let's get out of here."

I glanced to see who it was, and the tiny movement sent the tears spilling out onto my face. Elle spun me before Imogen could see. She wrapped a firm arm around me and walked with me, guiding me past the blurry shapes of people and toward the front gate.

"Not cool," Kyle said to Imogen, his voice carrying across the lawn and over the sound of the musicians still playing. His strong, pulsing magician energy flared as he turned to follow us.

I felt everything.

I felt Elle's static anger crackling next to me, and Kyle warming the air behind us, and the shock and concern and even smug satisfaction of the strangers who surrounded me. And I felt Imogen's hate boiling out, heavy and charcoal-black and laced with spite.

I could have pinned down the feelings of every last person there if the world hadn't been rushing in on me with such force that it was all I could do to keep walking. The crowd's emotions pressed against my skin and filled my ears with a dull roar.

I put one foot in front of the other. Elle's breathing beside me was a roaring wind. She held me tight, and I kept putting one foot in front of the other until the sounds started to fade. By the time we reached the end of Imogen's block, my heart-beat was louder than their collective feelings. When we were all the way to the next one, there was finally room in my head to think again.

"You guys didn't have to leave," I said.

My voice sounded dead to my own ears. Elle squeezed my shoulders.

"Imogen was a jerk," she said.

I laughed, though it seemed like the wrong response.

"I haven't told anyone else about that," I said. "I never, in a thousand years, thought she would tell anybody."

I hadn't realized we were that broken. And I hadn't imagined that realizing it would send me shattering into a thousand empathetic impressions.

My faerie side had taken over. I could almost hear the trees growing, and Elle and Kyle's magic shimmered so strongly I could see it faintly even through my glasses.

"You never thought she would tell *everybody*," Kyle said.

Elle frowned at Kyle. I didn't see her frown, but I knew she'd done it just the same.

"She said that in front of some people who really didn't need to know about it," I said. "And now they're going to talk."

"Memory spell?" Kyle suggested.

I snorted. One memory spell would be hard enough. Trying to glamour a whole yard full of competent Glims was a joke.

"You guys can go back," I said. "I'm okay." I took a deep breath and tried to force it to be true.

Elle rubbed my arm a little too briskly. The gesture was weirdly maternal.

"Give it up, godmother," she said.

Kyle slung an arm around my other side, reaching clear over my shoulder and around Elle. I was practically buried in his armpit, and the addition of him plus Elle's grip on my other side turned the three of us into an awkward animal lumbering down the sidewalk. But I didn't want them to move.

"You made us see each other," Kyle said. "Let us take care of you for two seconds."

He squeezed me in a one-armed, crushing hug.

The trees crackled and their magic shimmered around me. I wrapped my arms around my friends and let them hold me together.

CHAPTER EIGHTEEN

I pressed my fingertips against my temples. With my eyes closed and my forehead resting on my knees, the world was black, and I welcomed the darkness. The tree I leaned against pulsed with a slow, deep heartbeat, and its bark crackled softly as its uppermost branches swayed in the breeze.

The blades of grass beneath my feet grew, and the soil below them shifted with earthworms and other sheltered life. A dozen different messages filtered around me, carried by the wind—all the emotional litter the breeze had picked up from the city's Glims and their auras.

And that wasn't all. The emotions of every other person in this little park, Glim or Hum, rushed in on me. The girl sitting on a bench was worried about money. The middle-aged man felt existential fear about the trajectory of his life. The teenage wizard sitting on the other side of the park flared with anxiety every time his phone buzzed with a text, and somehow, without being told, I knew the text was from his boyfriend and that things weren't going well.

Beyond them, I felt the emotions of every person in every car that passed and I sensed the instincts of every squirrel and bird in the park.

I wanted to scream.

Instead, I let out a slow, steady breath and tried to shut everything out. I pushed back against the feelings and tried to imagine a tall, ten-foot-thick wall surrounding me, something that could keep all these sensations where they belonged.

But the more I tried to shut them out, the stronger the impressions grew. I couldn't pick out words, but the feelings were all too clear. Layers and layers of emotions pressed in on me, trying to smother me. Anger, fear, rage, sadness, stress, so much stress, a little flare of joy, and then fear and more fear again. It just kept coming. It would never end.

I'd managed to focus on Lily and school these past few days, anything to distract myself from memories of the stupid wedding and keep all this input at a distance. And then, this morning, I'd woken up to find every barrier and distraction had cracked and crumbled to the ground, leaving me bare.

I rocked back and forth, pressing my forehead into my denim-covered knees until it hurt.

"Stop," I ordered, not quite out loud. "Stop. Just stop. Shut up."

"Olivia?"

If the other voices had been loud, this one was a shout. I winced and let out another firm breath.

And then, everything fell silent. I stiffened, waiting for the emotions to rush in on me again. But nothing happened. The world felt frozen.

I looked up to see a pair of shifting green eyes staring at me with concern. Queen Amani crouched in front of me, her hand outstretched like she wasn't sure whether she should touch me.

"Are you okay?" she said. She kept her voice soft and low.

"Oh my god," I breathed. "Thank you."

I massaged my temples and closed my eyes again. The silence thrummed through me.

"Are you okay?" she repeated.

I didn't want her to talk. I just wanted to enjoy this endless quiet, where the only emotions I could feel were my own. But she was still staring at me, so I nodded.

"I'm fine," I lied. "Just overwhelmed."

She sat next to me and leaned her back against the tree. We were silent together for a few minutes. Someone walked by with their dog on a leash. I heard their footsteps, but that was all. I had no idea what they were feeling.

"How did you do that?" I said.

"You're wrapped up in my energy right now," Amani said. "You're safe. I've learned to block distractions."

"You'd have to."

We fell quiet again. Breaths rose and fell in my body. I rode them like waves, letting myself relax into the predictable rhythm.

"What's going on?" she said.

I ran a hand through my hair, brushing loose strands off my forehead.

"I don't know," I said. The relief of only feeling my own presence overwhelmed me. "It's been like this for days. I'll be fine and then everything just comes rushing in."

"And that's not normal for you?"

I shot a glance over at her. She seemed serious.

"No," I said slowly. "Why would it be?"

"Well, you're a faerie."

I snorted. "I'm a crappy faerie. Anyway, not all faeries deal with *this*."

I waved a hand around, trying to indicate literally everything in our general vicinity.

"Some of them do," she said.

"Then being a faerie sucks," I said.

She rested her head against the tree. Her curls pillowed around her dark face like a cloud.

"It's probably like anything else. Sucks sometimes, is awesome other times."

I closed my eyes again. I craved sleep.

"I just want to be normal," I said. The words came out so softly I didn't think she could hear them.

But Amani didn't need to hear me. If I was wrapped up in her energy, she felt what I felt, and she already knew.

Two women strolled by, one talking on her cell and the other trying to take a picture of the tree branches overhead while she walked. Amani watched them with her head tilted.

"When did this start?" she said.

I shrugged, though I knew exactly when. In a single moment, at Maia's wedding, every emotion in the neighborhood had crashed over my head. The feeling of being assaulted by the world had faded in and out for a few days. Now, the onslaught was becoming horribly familiar.

"I was at a friend's wedding," I said. "I got in a fight with... someone."

I didn't want to say Imogen's name in front of Amani again. I didn't want to say Imogen's name ever.

Amani tapped her knees with her fingers.

"That's why, then," she said.

"Having people be a nightmare to you means you can feel everything in the world?" My head snapped up. "Or did she curse me?"

A dozen swear words sprang to my lips, but I bit them back. The world didn't need more unnecessary noise.

Amani reached out a hand and felt the air around me. I knew she was sensing into my aura, and so I held still and tried to let her in. If anyone could figure out what was going wrong with me, it would be her. But she pulled her hand back.

"You're not cursed," she said. "You're just normal."

"This is not normal."

"You're normal for a faerie," she said. "And like it or not, you are a faerie." A sharp edge had crept into her voice.

Of course I annoyed her. Being a faerie had been her thing for decades. She was a professional Glim. I was probably her worst nightmare. I drew my legs up closer to my chest and stared at the ground in front of us.

I wished she'd go away and leave the silence behind her.

"Listen, how are you trying to shield yourself from all these impressions?"

I shrugged. "I don't know," I said.

A squirrel darted across the grass in front of us, too used to people to care that we were there.

"I'm just trying to keep them out. I visualized a wall, but it didn't do anything."

"That's half your problem," she said. "You're into science. You know Newton's Third Law, right?"

It sounded familiar, but not familiar enough. "I'm more into biology than physics," I said.

"'For every action, there is —'"

"'An equal and opposite reaction,'" I finished.

"Yup," she said. "So apply that to magic."

"What?"

She stared at me. "This, right here, is why I've pushed for free comprehensive magical education for elementary school students," she muttered. "Look." She twisted toward me. "That's what's going wrong. You're picking up all these energies, and you're pushing on them. So what are they going to do?"

"I don't know," I said.

"Yes, you do."

I watched the squirrel scamper up a tree.

"They're going to push back?"

"Bingo," she said. "You're swimming toward all the emotions you're trying to push away."

I pressed between my eyes, where a tension headache was starting to form.

"So what am I supposed to do? Just deal with them?"

"You've got to be like a boulder in a river," Amani said. "You have to plant yourself so firmly that you become part of the landscape. Make it easy for things to slip around you, and they will. Has no one ever taught you about grounding?"

"Mom has," I said. "And we used to practice it at Faerie Camp when I was a kid. But it never seemed to do anything."

"You were probably never dealing with enough energy that it made a difference," Amani said. "Until now, I mean. That fight you got into was probably pretty stressful, huh?"

"Yeah," I said.

She waited. I didn't elaborate.

"Stress lowers your immune system's response," Amani said. "And it lowers your aura's immune system, too. You probably just cracked wide open and everything you've been keeping out for years finally got a chance to rush in." She tilted her head. "Grounding is like, I don't know, wearing a surgeon's mask or taking antibiotics. It protects you most of the time, and builds your magical system back up when it gets strained."

"I've been stressed before," I said.

"But you had a support system, right? You were feeling okay about your life overall, or you had friends you could vent to?"

I nodded, though I wasn't sure.

"I'm guessing this time, you didn't have support. Home hasn't been too safe, or friends haven't had your back like you hoped."

I remembered the way the emotions had faded away after Elle and Kyle had rushed to protect and help me. I'd felt better with their arms around my shoulders.

"I think my parents are going to get divorced," I blurted.

The second the words were out, tears rushed up to follow them, prickling at my eyelids. I closed my eyes and breathed in and out, then in and out again. Amani put a hand on my knee. Warmth rushed into my body, and I couldn't tell if it came from her hand or her magic.

I hadn't even said the word aloud in my thoughts. I'd used *split up,* or *separate,* but never, ever *divorce.* The thought lined my stomach with lead and filled the lead with bile that sloshed around until I had to put my head back down on my knees to stop the nausea.

It should have been a good thought, with the way they fought. I should have been delighted. Maybe I'd get to live with my mom. Maybe I'd get out of talking to my dad until I was in my twenties and too old for him to say anything about my life and choices. There would be fewer people looking after me and Daniel, and we could live our own lives with less interference. Our parents would be so stressed out over trying to divide money and magical heirlooms and acquaintances that they wouldn't have time to make sure I attended a Glim university or that Daniel stopped sneaking away for his performance group.

They'd be too busy to have a family.

I couldn't catch my breath.

"Olivia." Amani's voice broke into my thoughts as though from a distance.

I forced my attention back to her. It was like trying to tame a wild animal.

She drew her knees up against her chest, too, and rested her chin on them with her head tilted so she could look at me.

"I'm sorry," she said.

"Me too."

"You need a shield," she said.

"From what, life?" I tried to laugh. Nothing came out except a raspy puff of air.

She tucked a gold-threaded curl behind her ear. "Home probably isn't the most relaxing place right now," she said.

I wiggled my toes, trying to tap the ground within the confinement of my shoes.

"I honestly haven't been there enough to tell you."

In between school, Wishes Fulfilled, Goose House, and the streets of Portland, home had turned into nothing more than a sleeping place. If I did get there during the day, I stayed in my room.

"Hold out your hand," Amani said. She held hers out, palm up, demonstrating.

I mimicked her.

She put her other hand over mine, palm down, close enough that I could feel heat. Our skin didn't touch, but the warmth between us grew until we may as well have been clasping hands. An overwhelming impression of silver filled my mind, the color glinting in the sun.

I closed my eyes to see better.

The image shifted and shimmered, and I caught sight of snaking emerald vines. They crept and twined around the edge of my field of vision, and slowly, as though a camera was focusing, the silver expanse shifted and resolved. The edges hardened to the shape of a vast shield.

Though I couldn't reach out and touch it, I felt the shield in my mind. Its sun-bright surface radiated heat, and the hot light wrapped around and enfolded me.

The tears prickling behind my eyes faded. Deep in the pit of my stomach, something grew calm and sturdy like a rock.

I took a deep breath.

Amani pulled her hand away. The image faded to blackness. Only my steady breathing remained.

EMMA SAVANT

"You're going to have to practice to keep it," she said. "But now you know what to aim for."

I tried to conjure up the shield again. Silver glittered at the edges of my vision, but it subsided too quickly. I tried again.

"Relax," Amani said.

I tried to let my mind and limbs loosen. A second later, the silver shimmers were back, stronger this time. They faded out.

"Once you get it up around your family, remember, don't push," Amani said. "Just hold it steady."

She put her fingertips on the ground and gently raised herself to a crouching position.

"I have to go," she said. "I'm going to be late for a Council meeting. Just keep practicing. I hope you get feeling better."

"Thanks," I said.

And then the sound on the world turned back up. She was gone, either whisked away by magic or moving too fast for my exhausted mind to keep up.

CHAPTER NINETEEN

I had never imagined a damp seashell could feel so hostile. I walked gingerly. Every step sent the shell thudding against my pocket and King Neptune's words ringing in my ears.

The shell had been on my desk this morning, set atop a crinkled piece of green paper with *Listen* written in blue ink. So I'd held it to my ear and listened.

Reprehensible conduct... heinous violation of the contract between land and sea... utter disrespect for authority... King Neptune Pacifica's voice had thundered in the privacy bubble I'd put up in my Wishes Fulfilled cubicle, making my ears ring.

And I'd ignored him.

I'd waited till the furious message fell to silence, then I'd put the shell in my pocket and headed out. Lorinda didn't need to deal with this one, and I felt too dead after that stupid wedding to care about anything King Pacifica had to say.

A small detour between Wishes Fulfilled and Goose House took me by the river. I pulled the seashell out of my pocket. It lay still and quiet in my palm. Its job was done; only the tiniest tendrils of magic clung to its swirling creamy surface.

A woman jogged along the path behind me. Emotions radiated off her, mostly worry. I waited until she was gone. Then, in one swift motion, I threw King Neptune's message as hard as I could.

The shell sailed through the air and landed in the dark gray water. A second later, it was gone. And then so was I, off toward Goose House.

A note on Lily's bedroom door said *Gone swimming!* Her new roommate, a faintly red half-goblin wearing a giant pink bow in her hair, pointed me down the hall.

"She's at the aquatic room," she said, her gravelly voice and Valley Girl inflections not quite blending together. Her emotions washed up toward me with the same mix of excitement and nerves that seemed to fill everyone at Goose House.

Lily's pale figure swam graceful laps in the small pool. Her pearly skin shimmered in the water and her hair streamed out behind her like a textured cape. A few other people were there, swimming laps or treading water or chatting quietly in the corner hot tub.

I sent a pulse of energy toward Lily, and she glanced up and then raced to the end of the pool, moving much faster than she should have been able to.

She hoisted herself up on the pool's edge. Water cascaded down from her body to the cement floor. She leaned back over the edge to squeeze water out of her hair.

"Breathing," she said, between heavy inhalations. "While swimming. *Hard.*"

"You looked good," I said.

"I'm getting the feel of it," she said. "This pool is shallow, though. Your relationship with water is so superficial. I need a…" She pursed her lips and lowered her eyebrows at me. "Aqualung," she finally said.

"Scuba?" I said.

"I guess?" she said. She grabbed a pale teal towel from a stack on the floor and wrapped it around her shoulders. "Anyway, hi," she said. "I'm so excited to see you. You were right, Evan's studio is amazing."

"I don't remember saying that," I said.

"But it is," she said. "I mean, I knew he had a gift, but—"

"But why do you know that?" I said, grabbing her arm. "Lily, did you go there?"

"Yes," she said breathlessly.

She had no idea I was mad at her. She couldn't see anything past the love-struck haze clouding her vision. I shook her arm.

"Lily," I said. "You can't do stuff like that."

Her delicate auburn eyebrows went up. She looked utterly quizzical, utterly innocent, and utterly like she needed a full-time babysitter.

"It wasn't difficult," she said. "I know where he works. My roommate showed me how to put his name into a computer and it told me. Goose House has a shuttle. I just had them drop me off in Oregon City and then they picked me up a while later. He gave me his business card, too. Now I have two of them!"

"What, are you going to start collecting them like Pokémon cards?" I said.

Of course, she didn't get the reference, and still didn't get why I was upset. I ran a hand through my hair.

"Lily, this is a really delicate situation. I know he's your true love and everything, but he also has a girlfriend and your dad is really mad at us right now. We need to go slow. We need to figure out if Evan's even on board with this before we go disrupting his life."

"Of course he's on board!" she said. "Godmother, he loves me!"

Lily had lucid moments where she made sense, where she seemed to be thinking things through and even making me reconsider my life choices.

And then she turned into this sparkly-eyed terror.

All her blathering about relationships and love had been the stupid foundation for attending that stupid, *stupid* wedding.

I dragged her out of the pool room.

"Human lesson time," I said. I needed a task to focus on. "You have to learn how land currency works. Among other things."

Once she had changed into a skirt and T-shirt and wrapped her damp hair up into coils on her head, I sat her down on the floor and pulled out my wand. I waved it and a stack of bills and coins shimmered into being.

"Whoa," Lily said.

"It's not real," I said. "Just an illusion. If you try to spend these, you'll get arrested."

I held out a handful of coins. She took them and bit her lip.

"These are your money, right?"

"This is Glim money," I said. "The little copper ones are called comets, the nickels are stars, the silvers are moons, and the gold ones are suns."

"Got it," she said. It wasn't hard to remember. Each coin had a picture of a trailing comet or crescent moon or whatever celestial body on both sides. I handed her another coin, this one silver with gold stars sprinkled across it.

"This one's a galaxy," I said. "Twelve of a small coin makes one of the coin above it. Like, twelve comets is a star."

"And twelve stars is a…" She furrowed her brow at the coins. "Moon."

"You got it. Why'd you go see Evan?"

She turned the galaxy over between her fingers. It glinted in the light.

"I'm here, aren't I?" she said. "Why waste time?"

"You're making my life harder," I said. "I'm going to try to get you together with Evan. I'm not sure I should, but I am. But you have a super delicate Archetype. Little Mermaids die sometimes. I heard of a Little Mermaid from about fifty years ago who was murdered by her prince's fiancée."

"Isabelle?" Lily said. Her eyes widened. "Isabelle won't kill me."

"How do you know that?" I said.

She laughed, because clearly this was all hilarious.

"Evan's told me about her, of course. She's terribly nice. That's why he's so hesitant about deepening our relationship. He doesn't want to hurt her. But he also doesn't feel like they have much chemistry, and he's worried he's settling."

"Why is he telling you this?" I said.

Not for the first time, the ambiguous morality of godparenting was not lost on me.

She shrugged. "We have a natural trust," she said. "He finds it easy to confide in me, probably because I'm his soulmate."

I held back a groan. I handed her a stack of bills.

"Take these," I said. "What are these?"

"No idea."

"So pay attention. This is Humdrum money."

She gazed at it, fascinated, as I explained how Humdrum money changed by country and how a comet was worth roughly fifty cents. Everything to do with humanity held her rapt, because everything to do with humanity had to do with the all-important Evan.

Once I'd drilled the coins and bills into her until she could recite them backwards, she put her hand on mine and looking imploringly into my eyes.

"I'll be careful," she said. "But godmother, please. I've waited my whole life for him. I can't slow down now. Love is about leaping."

"Yeah, overboard the ship with a dagger in your breast," I said. "That's how your Story goes, Lily. Godparents didn't even figure out to subvert it until the last hundred years. So please. Let me figure out the pace here, okay?"

She sighed and nodded. But I had a feeling her fingers were crossed behind her back, or at least would have been if that was a mermaid thing.

CHAPTER TWENTY

"I have to find some way to push Lily and Evan together in a way that doesn't feel fake," I said. "I can't hold their Story off forever."

"Isn't he still engaged, though?" Elle said. "If you ask me, Lily needs to go back into the ocean and learn to love herself before she tries loving anyone else. Especially someone who's already in a committed monogamous relationship."

I leaned back in my camping chair and met Elle's disapproving gaze. She was standing behind the table in the Pumpkin Spice's Saturday Market booth, rearranging sampler bags of coffee beans.

"I have to give them a chance to work this out on their own," I said. "That was the whole thing with your case, remember? It only worked out because I let you guys make your own decisions."

"You should just book her a photo shoot," Kyle said, from his camping chair next to me. "Then you can act all surprised when it turns out they know each other."

Elle froze, then muttered, "This could get awkward." She jerked her chin toward the front of the tent.

I recognized the girl who'd just turned into the booth, even though I hadn't seen her in months. The leonine cloud of auburn hair peeking from under her hood was hard to miss, as was the way she managed to look like a perfectly-curvy super-model even while wearing a boy's hoodie the exact gray of the wet pavement. Rain came down around her, a steady drizzle that hadn't stopped the rush of Saturday Market shoppers.

I cringed. I'd been practicing using Amani's shield to block the emotions of the dozens of people that wandered past us. But that got a lot harder when a distraction like this walked by.

Kyle sat in the Pumpkin Spice booth on the other side of Elle with his chair tipped back on two legs. He narrowed his eyes like he couldn't see the girl clearly.

"You met her at the street festival this last spring," I said, leaning over so I could keep my voice low. "The girl with Lucas?"

"Oh, yeah," he said, comprehension dawning in his voice and on his face at the same time.

He leaned back in the chair and stared until I kicked him under the coffee bean-laden table.

Aubrey was the girl who had dumped Lucas, and in turn sent Imogen and me into this downward spiral.

I hated her.

She tugged her hood down and buried her fingers in her hair and shook it out. The teasing gave her soft halo of curls movement it hadn't needed in the first place. Her steps further into the tent were fluid, her hips moving in a lazy figure-eight.

She, like Imogen, was a vivid reminder that I was not quite pretty, or sexy, or glamorous enough to be in Lucas' league. I could have saved myself a lot of pain by taking the reminder to heart a little earlier.

I tried to pull up the shield Amani had tried to teach me, to keep all these icky feelings from getting to me. Silver shimmered across my vision and a hint of an emerald vine unfurled in a bottom corner, but then they started fading in and out. I couldn't concentrate enough. I let the vision go and watched out of the corner of my eye as Aubrey perused the bags of gourmet coffee beans lined up on little wooden racks. Only half of them were meant for Humdrums like Aubrey. Her eyes slid over the sparkling Glim bags like they weren't even there.

Months ago, she'd gone prom dress shopping with Imogen and me and spent the whole time offering backhanded compliments that made me sure I never wanted to see her again. A glamour would hide me well enough; I had my hand halfway up to where my wand was buried in my hair before her gaze landed on me. Then it was too late.

"Oh my god, hi!" she said. "How's it going? Haven't seen you in a while."

She went to a different school than me. I took a split second to feel grateful.

"Yeah, busy summer," I said.

Go away, I thought, but she was no faerie and didn't pick up on the hostility that practically radiated out of my pores.

She put her hands in her pockets, slouching like a photographer had ordered her to.

"You look familiar," she said to Kyle.

"We've seen each other," he said. "But never met."

He held out a hand, and she shook it. Above her surface-level smile, her sharp eyes took him in as though trying to figure out if he was worth her time. Apparently he wasn't, so she turned to me.

She gazed at me just a second too long. "So," she said. "I heard Imogen ripped you a new one."

I flipped through my mental files, trying to imagine how she could possibly know that, seeing as how neither she nor Lucas were at the wedding and she and Imogen were hardly on speaking terms. I came up with nothing.

Even her emotions were no help. She was slightly annoyed and totally full of herself, as always.

"How'd you hear that?" Kyle asked for me.

"Imogen's cousin goes to my school," she said. She had a low, slow voice, the kind of voice that had nowhere to be and knew no one was going to interrupt. "Screaming match at a wedding? Word gets around."

Great. Now even the Humdrums were talking about me. And my parents' marriage, probably. The thought of the story reaching my mom or dad made my stomach practically fold in on itself.

"Everyone will be over it in a week," Aubrey said. "Seriously, whose parents aren't on the verge of breaking up? It's kinda weird that yours are still together, to be honest."

"So are mine," Kyle said, frowning at her.

She waved him off. "Again, weird," she said.

A silence fell. I couldn't tell whether it was awkward or not. I felt uncomfortable around her as a rule; whether she ever felt the same way about anything was another question.

I let the silence drag, hoping she'd get the hint and go. But she just stood there, watching us and calmly waiting for someone to speak.

Fine. I'd check the small talk boxes. Then she could go away and never bother me again.

"So, how have you been?" I said.

I couldn't have made my voice more fake and cloying if I'd tried.

A tiny smirk bent the corners of her mouth. "You mean about Lucas, right?"

I hadn't, exactly, but she went there anyway.

"He was an idiot to let go of me that quickly, to be honest," she said. "I tried texting him the other day and all he said was, 'I'm with Imogen now.' I was just checking in to be sure he was okay, but I swear he thought I was trying to *seduce* him or something."

I couldn't imagine saying something like that as matter-of-factly as she did. It must be a whole different world, thinking that highly of yourself.

"But it's cool," she said. She examined her nails. "I'm dating a guy now who is *much* better for me. He's in college, so, you know. We have more in common."

"I thought you were in high school," Kyle said.

"I am."

"So how does him being in college mean you have more in common?"

She stared at him for a moment, then twitched her head as though shaking off a fly and turned back to me.

"Having said that, his shiny new girlfriend is still an interfering bitch. So what are you going to do about it?"

The idea that it was my job to do something about it hadn't even crossed my mind. Aubrey face was tense but expectant.

She actually thought I had a plan.

All I could manage was a shrug, which was not at all what she'd been looking for.

"Don't tell me you're just going to roll over like a puppy," she said.

It was amazing how someone whose opinion I cared about so little could make me so instantly eager to justify myself. I bit the inside of my cheek to keep from leaping to my own defense.

"I don't see how Imogen's my problem," I said instead. *Take the high road, Feye.*

"Imogen is everyone's problem," Aubrey said. Her emotions flared, and this time, I felt something sharp embedded in her self-interest. "Look, I didn't do anything about her because if Lucas wanted to ditch me for someone as skanky as that, you know, let him have her."

She raised one ring-studded hand into the air and flicked it, like she was washing her hands of the whole thing.

"But you didn't do anything to Imogen, and she was a megabitch to you at that wedding. My cousin's friend's sister told me all about it. And I want to know if you're going to take that from her or if Imogen Dann gets to run the whole world like some pathetic princess."

It was hard to tell how much of my thoughts were mine and how much were Aubrey's. Ever since the wedding, taking on other people's feelings had become as easy as slipping on a coat. Now, outrage—barely suppressed as it was—coiled up inside me, ready to strike.

I took a deep breath and tried to untangle whatever was hers from whatever was mine. But it was hard, because while she was angry, I agreed completely. Imogen was an entitled monster, and, while she was not technically a princess even in our world, she was acting like the worst of them.

I didn't like Aubrey. But that didn't mean she didn't make sense. We were definitely on the same page when it came to how evil Imogen was.

"I don't know," I said.

I was *still* taking Imogen's crap, like I had for our whole friendship. After I'd gotten over licking my wounds, I'd even been willing to forgive her for lying to me and stealing a guy before I even had a shot with him, because I was either a saint or a doormat, I wasn't sure which.

But Imogen Dann had crossed a line when she'd started shouting about my family.

Aubrey sighed. She picked up a bag of beans and flipped it over, eyes scanning the label without seeming to see it.

"Whatever," she said. "Obviously I'm talking to a wall. Have a good week."

She flashed a smile that barely made it to her cheeks, let alone her eyes, and left, her effortless slouch turning the path out of the booth into a catwalk. She threw her hood up. The grey hid her hair like water dousing a candle.

I felt her expectation as she walked off, like she was maybe waiting for one of us to come after her. None of us moved.

Elle waited a tactful five seconds before speaking. "Yikes," she muttered.

Kyle had grown tense beside me.

"You're not going to listen to that, are you?" he said, his voice lined with concern.

I took a deep breath and turned to face him. "Of course not," I said.

I blew a long stream of air out between my lips, then smirked as a thought occurred to me that would have been a whole lot more help months ago.

"I don't know why I was ever so upset about Lucas," I said. "He dated that—" I jerked my head toward Aubrey "—followed immediately by Imogen. What does that say to you?"

Elle laughed, but Kyle's face stayed blank, so I spared him the trouble of answering.

"Lucas has a thing for crazy girls with drama problems," I said. I felt myself relax for the first time in days. It was almost funny. "And he doesn't like me like that. And I just realized—I should be *flattered*."

And that was true. But it didn't stop Aubrey's words from ringing in my ears long after I'd left for home.

CHAPTER TWENTY-ONE

A year ago, work had been a drag—a thing that tied me down to the Glimmering world and wasted time I could have spent on my garden or in the forest or doing just about anything not related to my aggravating faerie-ness.

These days, at least when I wasn't dealing directly with Lily and her ethical gray areas, Wishes Fulfilled almost felt like a sanctuary. I could clock in, shuffle papers around for Tabitha, and clock out, all without having to think about anything important.

I wasn't sure if word of Imogen's outburst had reached my family; I hadn't let myself go home long enough to find out. It had been a couple of weeks since the wedding, and I'd managed to be gone during dinner every single day. I'd be gone again tonight; I'd decided to take Lily out to give her dining skills a test run.

Rain pounded on the windows. The first week of October had hit in usual Portland style, with heavy gray clouds and rain that never let up for more than a few minutes. This was a rougher downpour than usual, and I liked being in my warm, well-lit cubicle while the world stormed on by outside. I was so zoned in on the comfort of organizing Tabitha's calendar for the next week that I didn't even hear Lily come in.

"Hi!" she said, way too loudly.

I yelped and shot backward, the wheels of my chair a little too willing to roll across the polished wood floor. My seat bounced against the scratchy cubicle wall, making it vibrate.

Lily's eyes were as round as two sand dollars.

"I'm so sorry!" she said. "Oh my goodness, are you all right? I didn't mean to scare you!"

My heart slammed around inside my ribcage. I took a few deep breaths.

"You're fine," I said. "I was kind of focused." I frowned. "I thought I was picking you up. How did you get here?"

"Bus," she said.

Her face practically glowed with pride, and I had to admit that riding a bus across town was probably a pretty big deal if you'd spent your life in a river.

I waved at the ugly plastic yellow chair that had somehow found its home in the corner of my cubicle. A paper airplane fluttered past, high over our heads.

"Good job," I said. "Pull up a seat."

She dragged it over and sat, her toes grazing the ground. She pressed her knees together and bounced them up and down while her hands tried to hold them still. She waited all of two seconds before launching in.

"I need you to perform a love spell," she said.

I caught my breath in a hurry.

"Absolutely not," I said. "Those are the worst."

I knew, because I'd done one in the spring for Elle. It had been a nightmare for everybody.

"But I need you to!" she said. "Evan won't leave his girl-friend!"

I held up a hand.

"Whoa," I said. "How do you know? I thought we were going to go visit Evan again *together* once you had your legs under you a little more."

That had been the plan. Her face made it clear that the plan had not been followed. Again.

I couldn't even pretend to be surprised.

"I couldn't help myself," she said.

I felt like she should look a little more apologetic than she did. Whatever guilt she felt was overlaid by the kind of rapture I was coming to identify as Evan Face.

"I love him so much and I just had to go see him," she said. "We were talking on the *internet* together. Don't look at me like you don't approve, because I already know you don't. We began sharing our fondness for one another and I couldn't bear to be away from him for a moment longer. So I went to see him, and oh, faerie godmother, it was wonderful!"

She sighed and closed her eyes, looking way too blissed-out to be talking about some dude.

"I love him," she repeated, which—shockingly enough— was not news to me. "We had such a lovely conversation, and I told him I have feelings for him, and he said he has feelings for me, too, but he also said that he's committed to his girlfriend and can't betray her trust."

"Good," I said, but Lily was too far gone to listen.

"And so I need you to perform a spell that will make him realize he loves me, not her."

Her eyes were bigger than a puppy's. I folded my arms across my chest and tried to figure out how to explain to her that really, really wanting something wasn't always a good enough reason to get it. Especially not when it involved dragging me into the middle of things.

"I need this, faerie godmother!" she said. "I can't tell you how much I need it!"

"Olivia," I corrected.

She was too busy clasping her hands to her bosom to hear me.

She hadn't been this bad in a while. I couldn't decide whether I liked her earnestness or just wanted to strangle her. The scales were tipped strongly in the strangling direction when she added, "Also, I need a new place to live. Your boss says I can't be at Goose House anymore."

I'd been enjoying the day. I'd been holed up, feeling cozy, and so of course everything had to start imploding.

And I wasn't in the mood.

I stood up and marched past Lily and out of my cubicle. One of my coworkers, Aster, stopped typing and watched me pass, but I ignored her.

Lorinda's blinds were pulled up. I could see her and Tabitha through the glass windows, sipping tea and talking about the papers on Lorinda's desk. The dark purple walls loomed over them.

Tabitha's back was to me, so all I could see was the back of her severe black bob and her black shawl. She looked more like a stylish French witch than a faerie godmother, which, on days of less crisis, gave me a tiny bit of hope that I could manage this job for a bit without falling prey to the horrible pastel suits Lorinda seemed to love.

Lorinda had barely called "Come in" before I entered.

I kept one hand on the door frame for support. This had seemed like a better idea until I was actually standing here with their eyes on me.

"Do you have a minute?" I said.

Lorinda raised her eyebrows at me. "Looks like I'd better," she said. "Tabitha, pardon me."

They both turned to me and waited.

I took a deep breath.

"My client is in my cubicle," I said. "Apparently you told her she can't stay at Goose House."

Lorinda frowned and sighed deeply. The shoulder pads under her sky-blue blazer rose and fell with the breath.

"I certainly didn't expect her to come here," she said.

"So what's the problem?" I said. "Why can't she stay at Goose House?"

"I was trying to convince her to go back to the river where she belongs," Lorinda said.

She glanced at Tabitha, then back at me.

"King Pacifica has been exerting a certain amount of pressure and I hoped that if she didn't have a place to stay, she might be more willing to give this up and go home."

"I thought the Oracle had approved this," Tabitha said.

"The Oracle doesn't have to deal with daily messages from Neptune threatening he'll press kidnapping charges," Lorinda said grimly. "If it's the girl's choice, the Oracle can't say anything about it. Even the Oracle is required to accept our clients' choices about their Stories."

"Being required to accept them doesn't mean she does," Tabitha said, but Lorinda shot her a quelling look.

I drummed my fingers on the doorframe.

"Next time, I would *really* appreciate if you would let me know," I said, trying and—judging by the amusement on Tabitha's face—failing to be polite.

Lorinda sighed in a way that made me think I wasn't the only one having a bad day.

"I'm sorry, Olivia," she said. "I should have mentioned it."

"What do I do now?" I said. "She can't stay at my place."

My parents would never go for it. Or worse, they might *really* go for it and see making Lily welcome as a way to nurture my fledgling godmother career, and that wasn't happening.

"What about your friend?" Lorinda said. "Imogen?"

"No," I said.

"The Danns might have room," Tabitha said. "Didn't her parents just have one of their daughters get married? I'm sure they'd have space for Lily for a week or two."

"No," I repeated. "Lily cannot stay with Imogen."

"Imogen's a nice girl," Lorinda said. "Her supervisor speaks very highly of her."

"Her supervisor clearly doesn't know Imogen cheated on her Proctor Exam," I said.

The blood rushed hot to my face the second the words left my lips.

The silence congealed in the air, almost thick enough to reach out and touch. Lorinda pursed her lips, and Tabitha's dark eyebrows tightened. They glanced at each other, and then Tabitha looked at me and cocked her head, waiting.

"I didn't say that," I said.

But then, why not?

Imogen had cheated. And Aubrey was right: My former best friend was going to keep acting like she ran the world if no one ever called her on her crap.

The Oracle said I could use Imogen's secrets however I wanted, that telling the truth about her would mean "balance in my world." I wasn't dumb enough to think that balance meant we'd be friends again like nothing had ever happened. But we were never going to be friends again anyway. Imogen had made that clear.

Maybe I'd feel better about it and be able to let this whole stupid thing go.

"That's a fairly serious accusation," Tabitha said, her voice gentle as though she didn't want to spook me. But I wasn't in the mood to be spooked.

"Ask the Oracle if you don't believe me," I said.

They could take it from here. I turned back to Lorinda. "So what am I supposed to do?"

She rubbed the place between her eyes. "Lily can stay the rest of the month," she said. "I'll call and arrange it. But you need to have this case wrapped up by the end of October."

"I can do that," I said.

I frowned, not sure where those words had come from. I had no idea if I could do that. But the look on Lorinda's normally brisk face was so exhausted that I knew I'd have to make it work.

I tapped the doorframe. "Thank you. Seriously."

She offered me a tired smile, and I left, closing the door quietly behind me.

CHAPTER TWENTY-TWO

The tiny rooftop garden a few buildings away from Wishes Fulfilled was overgrown with weeds and climbing flowers. It was supposed to be a community garden for local Glims, but no one kept up on it. A lone picnic table sat in a corner, its dark reddish-brown paint peeling with age. Lily and I sat on top of the table with our feet resting on the bench. Lily bounced her legs absently, making the table vibrate. Rain fell around us, but we were dry and warm under the protective bubble I'd created.

"I can't remember what it's called," Lily said. "It's on the computer. There's a place where you write questions, and then it gives you the answers. It's how I found Evan that one time."

"A search engine?" I said.

"Um, sure," Lily said.

She twirled a strand of green-threaded hair around her finger.

"So I asked it how I could find Evan Costner, and then I clicked on some blue letters that had his name. And that took me to this different computer screen. And then all his pictures were there. And it was strange, because they were all images he'd taken, but none of them were of him." She sighed. "It made me miss him, so I messaged him. I long for him."

"Yeah, I know," I said.

I felt the waves of beautiful desperation pour off of her, an endless rush of wanting something she seriously shouldn't have.

"You still disapprove," she said.

I tapped my knees with my palms.

"Honestly?" I said. "Who cares if I disapprove? You don't care. Your dad doesn't care. My boss doesn't care. I'm not sure who I'm trying to impress."

She frowned. "You sound bitter."

"It's not bitter," I said, and let out a huge gust of air, trying to let some of my tension go with it. "It's just, I'm tired. I've been dealing with a lot lately, and I don't have a lot of energy to worry about whether you're making the right decisions, especially since you don't seem to be interested in my advice anyway. No offense, but let's be honest, you're not."

"Not when it comes to Evan," Lily said.

She had the good grace to look slightly ashamed. She studied the wet ground and wrapped her hands around her knees.

"I respect you as a godmother, I really do. But I can't let anyone else make decisions for me when it comes to Evan. He's my everything."

I knew. I bit back another sigh.

"You're in luck," I said. "I've already booked that photo shoot with him. We're going to go there together and you're going to get head shots taken."

Her eyebrows furrowed. "Head shots?"

Nervousness tingled from her, and it took me a second to realize why.

"Not like someone's shooting you in the head," I said. "Head shots are pictures of your face. People get them for their online portfolios and professional social media pages and stuff. And actors get them when they're trying to get roles. We could always tell him you're an actress."

Her hand flew to the back of her neck.

"I'd love to be an actress!" she said. "Then we could both be in the arts. He could take pictures and I could be *in* the moving pictures. Wouldn't that be romantic?"

"Movies," I said. "They're called movies."

"When are we head shooting?" she said. "Please say soon."

"Soon-ish," I said.

I bit the inside of my cheek and debated on my next words, but decided to be honest. It wasn't like Lily would care anyway.

"He's gone half of this week because he's taking his girl-friend to a show in Seattle for her birthday."

No reaction, other than breathless anticipation. A little gray bird skittered to a stop on the ground a ways in front of us. Water beaded on its feathers. It froze for a second and then fluttered into the air again before diving into the tiny potting shed that held unused tools.

"After he gets back from Seattle, he's booked for a while," I said. "So two Tuesdays from now, we'll go see him."

She clasped her hands to her chest, like I'd thought people only did in silent films from the twenties.

"Oh, faerie godmother!"

"Olivia," I said automatically, but she wasn't listening.

"When is he leaving for Seattle?"

"I have no idea," I said. "I only got that much information because I pried like a creeper."

"If we go right now, I imagine we could see him," Lily said. "We could tell him that we wanted to come discuss the details of the head shots before we actually do them, and then we could actually go do them at our appointment. Please. I'll die if I don't see him again soon!"

I waited until the melodramatic torrent dried up and then blinked at her.

"Seriously?" I said.

"I'm ready," Lily said. "We both are. We need to see each other. Our last conversation didn't end well."

"By which you mean he wouldn't abandon his probably long-term girlfriend for you," I said.

"What if he forgets about me? What if he spends all that time with her and then doesn't want to come home to me?"

"Then he's probably a good person," I said.

She groaned. It was a desperate, raw sound, something I hadn't heard come out of her before. The frustration that often seemed to fritz around her aura swelled into a tangible rush.

"There's so much we don't know about each other," she said. "How are we supposed to be married if you won't even let us talk? He doesn't even know I'm a mermaid!"

That had to stop, right here, right now. I put a firm hand on hers.

"He can't know that," I said.

The nightmare of trying to explain that one not just to Lorinda but to magical law enforcement threatened to engulf me.

"Lily?" I said. "Listen. There are laws about that.'

"You land people don't follow laws," she said. "They're just suggestions to you. I know all about 'speed limits.'"

I squeezed her hand, hard.

"I'm not talking about speed limits," I said. "You cannot tell him you're a Glim."

A slight breeze rushed down between the buildings and into our courtyard. It was cool and made the hair on the back of my neck stand on end; I hoped it was doing the same thing to Lily to reinforce the gravity of her situation.

"Hum-Glim relationships don't always turn out well," I said. "I know you love Evan. I get that. But magic is a big thing for a Humdrum to just come to terms with. I mean, can you imagine if you started dating someone and then they told you that an entire world existed under your nose that you knew nothing about?"

Lily smiled at me like I was an idiot child.

"Olivia," she said gently. "Evan *did* show me a new world. Evan *is* my new world!"

I didn't smack her.

"It's not like that," I said. "It's not like, 'Yay, there's an amazing new world full of magic, let's get married!' A lot of the time, the Hums aren't happy. One partner having magic is a lot of inequality to throw into a relationship. I had this friend."

The word *friend* seemed wrong on my tongue. Ex-friend? Former bestie? What was Imogen, anyway?

"Her aunt was dating this Hum guy," I said. "They decided to get married. And so he gave her a ring, and then she told him she was a faerie. And he said he was fine with it. But whenever she'd use a spell, he'd make a snide comment about how it was a shame things weren't that easy for everyone. Or whenever she tried to introduce him to her Glim friends, he'd make a big deal about how he didn't have any special powers."

She looked at me. I couldn't tell if she was listening.

"It wore their relationship to pieces," I said. "They broke up and they had to glamour his memories. He doesn't remember our world now; he just remembers that their relationship went sour and that she gave the ring back."

"The ring," Lily said. "That's part of the law, right?"

"You can't tell someone you're Glim until you've exchanged a serious token of your relationship, like an engagement ring or an apartment key or something," I said. "You have to enchant the token with a spell so the Council can track down the Hum if they need to glamour their memory. People break up so often that glamouring memories is part of the law."

"That won't be a problem for Evan and me," Lily said. "Our love can withstand anything."

"Most mixed relationships fail," I said.

"Ours will last forever," she said.

I rubbed the spot between my eyes. Another bird cawed as it hopped along edge of the rooftop.

"So you keep telling me," I said. "You know what? Whatever. Maybe it will. Just, please, stop trying to force it until after your photo session with him, okay?"

"Oh, thank you, faerie godmother!" she said.

She didn't make any promises.

"Come on," I said. My skin practically itched with a need to change the subject. "Let's get dinner and see if you remember how Humdrum money works."

CHAPTER TWENTY-THREE

Lily managed to eat and pay for an entire plate of spaghetti without letting anyone in the tiny Italian restaurant know she was a mermaid. I decided to take her for drinks after to celebrate.

"Think about it, though," I said.

We sat at a table at the underage Glimmering nightclub, Gilt. Floating vanilla candles in holders made of shimmering autumn leaves floated above our heads, giving the air a soft warm scent at odds with the pulsing music and flashing lights on the dance floor. I'd thrown up a sound shield so we could talk without shouting.

"Winter is almost here," I said. "And you could either be here, in Portland, freezing your legs off, or you could be swimming to Hawaii."

"Been there, done that," she said.

I couldn't imagine how someone could sound that bored when it came to Hawaii in October. She sipped her sparkling water laced with sea spray and pomegranate.

"I want to move on with my life, faerie godmother. I want Evan."

"But maybe Evan doesn't want you," I said.

I'd given up on using any conversation more delicate than a blunt instrument with her.

"He's engaged to another woman," I said, slowly and clearly. "And he's committed to her. He chats online with you and has little secret meetings with you here and there. You're a secret. Meanwhile, he takes her out to lunch with his friends. He wants to spend his life with her."

"I want him to take me to lunch," she said. "He's perfect."

"I'm sure he's a catch." I rolled my eyes. "But maybe he's not your catch, especially if he's the kind of guy who cheats on people. There are plenty of other fish in the sea. Where you live."

"Where I lived," she corrected. "I don't know why you helped me get legs if you were only going to try to make me go back."

"Because I'm bad at my job," I said.

I stared down into my lavender lemonade. Two glasses scented with the calming herb hadn't done anything to keep my temperature from spiking every time I thought about going through with setting my client up with her One True Love. Our arguments on both sides were getting a little thin around the edges, with no sign of either of us wearing the other down.

I propped my head on my hand and looked out at the dance floor. It was a jumble of swirling bodies in weird clothes. Their magic rose in clouds outside the edges of my glasses, but even looking straight through them, the cobweb shawls and color-changing unicorn-hair dresses made it clear this wasn't your average crowd. That might have had something to do with the tiny red dragon coiled around a sorcerer guy's neck, though. It spat a stream of gold sparks into the hair of the elf dancing beside it.

"I have a question for you, on a totally different subject," Lily said. She was a little too enthusiastic, probably trying to make me feel better about this whole thing. "I've been hearing stuff about that Oracle you mentioned."

"Yeah?" I said.

Even though I'd told her more than once that the Oracle was on her side, this was the first time she'd seemed interested. It wasn't surprising. Even the Faerie Queen didn't have much to do with the magic in the ocean, so it was possible that Lily had barely even heard of other Glimmering leaders. The sea had rules and leaders of its own.

"I heard a few people at Goose House mention her, so I thought I'd learn more," she said. "It seems I can still communicate with other water creatures quite easily, even though I'm technically human now."

She put just enough emphasis on the "human" to remind me that she wasn't planning on giving that up anytime soon.

"So I contacted the water sprites that live in the Oracle's Fountain."

I sat up. I'd heard of people talking to the sprites, of course. They handled most of the Oracle's business and lived in her fountains all around the city. Imogen had asked them for enchanted water or advice dozens of times. But the way Lily said it, I got the impression she'd called them up just to *chat*.

"Let me tell you, they had something to say," Lily said. "They're complete gossips. And I have no idea why you are all so obedient to the Oracle. She sounds kind of, well…" She leaned in and whispered, "Rude."

"Rude," I repeated.

The Oracle could be a little distant sometimes, sure, but that was because she was, well, the Oracle. Not all the leaders of our world could be as friendly as Queen Amani.

Lily had so much to learn. The concept of teaching it all to her made the spot between my eyes hurt.

"I thought you were focused on getting along with the Humdrums here," Lily said. "My father said everyone on land is practically obsessed with fitting in with the Humdrums and not disrupting their world. But the Oracle isn't like that. Why? And why do you all still respect her so much if she's harassing the Humdrums and you're all trying to keep them from knowing you exist?"

My spine prickled.

"What do you mean?"

But I already knew. It hit me like the ceiling had come crashing in on my head.

I fought to keep my face steady.

Did Amani know?

She sat up straighter and wrapped her hand tightly around her glass.

"Is this not common knowledge?" she said. "I thought maybe it was a secret because of the way the sprites talked about it, but I figured *you'd* know. I mean, you work across the street from her Fountain."

"Is what not common knowledge?" I said. "What would I know?"

She stared at me.

"The Oracle," she said. "She's been pulling pranks and things on the Humdrums, or paying people who do it for her. Trying to scare them, I guess, make them think it's ghosts. I was wondering why. I thought you knew."

"No, I didn't," I said.

I touched the silver ring through my shirt. It felt hot, or maybe that was just my nerves. Goosebumps rose up all along my arms.

"Why would she make them think it's ghosts?" I said. I kept my voice as calm and smooth as the surface of a still lake.

"I don't know," Lily said. "That's what I was curious about."

I rolled my lips together, forcing my breathing to stay steady, unwilling to get too far ahead of myself too soon.

"What else did you hear?" I said. "I need to know everything, Lily. This could be, like, super important."

She swirled her faintly pink drink around in her glass. Tiny crystalline bubbles rose to the surface and popped.

"She's been giving rewards to people who do things to scare Humdrums," she said. "She can tell who does it, because she can practically watch the whole city. She can see through any bit of clean water, obviously."

"Wait, *what?*" I said.

She squinted at me, like she wasn't sure she was seeing me clearly, like no one could possibly be this stupid.

"It doesn't have to be big," Lily said. "There are mermaids who can do the same thing, sometimes. I can if I focus really, really hard. That's how I contacted her sprites. I thought you knew that."

"Nope," I said.

250

"Weird. Well, she's good at it—like, she can see anything through raindrops or puddles or fountains or the river or, well, anything."

I shoved my lemonade away so hard it sloshed over the edge of the glass. My heart pounded. Lily's eyebrows knit together in concern until she realized why, and then she shook her head and pushed the glass back toward me.

"Clean water," she repeated. "That's got lemon and stuff in it. It would be like trying to look through a mirror covered in mud."

That didn't mean no one around us was drinking water, or hadn't tracked in a puddle from their shoes and coat. I glanced around, suddenly grateful I'd put the sound shield up not only to protect us from the pulsing dance music but to protect our conversation from any prying ears, too.

I put both hands around my glass anyway, trying to shield the liquid. I'd never felt so distrustful of lemonade.

Outside our shield, the music throbbed and pulsed. My heartbeat raced to catch up with it.

"What kinds of rewards?" I said. "Who's been scaring Humdrums?"

I didn't even know if these were the right questions. I rubbed the ring through my shirt fabric. Should I take Lily to Amani now or wait until I'd squeezed every bit of information from her?

I couldn't imagine what the consequences would be if I accused the Oracle of something like this.

"She pays them in gold, mostly," she said. "That's what the Oracle traffics in, isn't it? And wishes." She paused and tilted her head. "Does the Oracle really grant wishes? Like the Sea Witch?"

"Kind of like that," I said.

"I heard she started doing it for Glimmering teenagers who liked to pull pranks on the Humdrums for a laugh. And then word caught on, and she's got a lot of people coming to her now, telling her what they did and making sure she or her sprites saw it. People get the biggest rewards if they can get Humdrums to move out of their buildings. I don't think that's very nice, but the sprites say that's the game."

"Do they know why?" I said.

She shrugged. Her pearly shoulder peeked out from her slouchy pink sweater.

"It doesn't sound like the Oracle lets them in on much," she said. "They just do whatever she says because, well, she's the boss."

My hands felt cold. I pressed them between my knees to keep them from trembling.

"What else do people do?"

"I don't know," she said. She looked faintly surprised, like she hadn't expected so much attention. "I could find out, if you want. I think they just try to scare Humdrums or get reactions out of them. But I don't know why. That's why I was asking."

"I'm glad you did," I said.

I propped my elbows on the table and let my head fall into my hands. My skull felt impossibly heavy. Or maybe that was my brain, loaded down with all this new information. It held more than I wanted to know.

The world felt too big sometimes, and I didn't know where I fit in it. What had started as a not-awesome summer job had turned into a job I kind of liked, but even that seemed to be rapidly turning into something that was way over my head.

Why couldn't anything be simple?

I let out a long, slow breath and tried to think.

Immediately, the emotions and thoughts of a dozen people all flooded into my brain, pushing against each other like the crowd on the too-small dance floor. The girl from the next table over was depressed because her best friend had just moved across the country. I didn't know how I knew that—I just knew, the same way I knew the guy across the table from her was stressing over how to tell her he liked her sister, and the same way I knew the crazily-dancing sprite at the closest edge of the dance floor was only shaking her body all over the place because she didn't want to think about how badly she was doing in math class.

I sat straight up, slamming doors in my mind and shoving all the people out with a wall of silver.

I hadn't invited them. I hadn't done anything to let them in except have the audacity to try to clear my head for one second so I could figure out what to do next.

I'd been getting better at using Queen Amani's shield, but I wasn't good enough. A couple of days ago, I'd been sitting in class, minding my own business and taking notes for a literature test, when the emotions of every person in the room had come streaming into my head. I'd had to excuse myself to the nurse's office, claiming a migraine.

Every time, it was exactly like it had been at the wedding: One moment, everything was normal. The next, I was fighting for space inside my own mind.

Lily leaned in toward me, her eyes open and too close to mine.

"Are you okay?" she said. Her voice was way too loud.

I shut my eyes and held out a hand, trying to make myself as steady as a boulder and let the last lingering impressions slip out of my headspace.

When I opened my eyes, she was still gaping at me.

"It's nothing," I said. "Faerie problems."

I pushed my glasses up on my nose and rubbed the spot between my eyes. The music pulsed at the edges of our bubble.

"I need to go make a call," I said. "I'll be right back."

I pushed up from the table. The ring burned my skin.

I pulled a couple of coins from my pocket and put them on the table.

"Go ahead and get another drink if you want. I'll be back in ten minutes, okay?"

The music thundered behind me as I flew down the stairs and out into the street. The perpetual autumn rain had let up, leaving the pavement shining with puddles dyed red and yellow with reflections of the streetlight down the block.

I walked quickly toward the corner, pulling my phone out as I walked. I pulled up my mom's last message.

Olivia: I'll be home late. Project for work.

Silently, I made a wish that she wouldn't care. I couldn't deal with more parent drama on top of all this.

I sent a pulse of magic down the first dark alleyway I came to. It ricocheted off the Dumpster at the far end and bounced back, its echo letting me know there was no one there but me and a couple of Humdrum rats.

I pulled Amani's silver ring from under my shirt. It seemed to throb in my hands. I scanned the ground. Puddles glinted darkly from every direction.

If the Oracle was spying through the water, she'd picked the right city.

I crouched and pulled my wand from my hair. A second later, a jet of fire poured out the tip of my wand. I pointed the enchanted flames at the ground around me, then at the walls on either side.

That would have to be good enough. I shoved the wand back in my hair, threw up a sound bubble, and slipped the ring onto my pinkie finger with the tiny mirror in the band facing toward me.

The ring glowed gold for a moment, then Queen Amani's minuscule face appeared in its surface. The image was clear and bright, the only spot of light in the alley.

"Olivia," she said, and she sounded both pleased and alarmed. "I haven't heard from you in a while. Are you okay?"

"I need to talk to you," I said. "As soon as possible. I was just talking to my client and—"

I fell silent. Even alone, even with my protection spell, I could swear the brick walls on either side of me were listening in.

"It's sensitive," I said. "We need to talk somewhere safe."

"Of course," she said instantly, cutting me off. "Where are you?"

"Close to Burnside Bridge," I said.

"Meet me at the bus station by the bridge," she said. "I'll be there in ten minutes."

"I'll be there in fifteen," I said. "I have to send my client home."

She nodded and our connection winked out. The darkness closed in on me, leaving a glowing afterimage of her face floating in my vision.

I shoved the ring back under my shirt and walked back to Gilt as fast as I could without running.

Lily wasn't at the table. I couldn't see anything through the colored lights and pulse of the dancers on the floor, so I nudged my glasses down my nose and sent out a green tendril of magic. These little spells were coming to me easier than they had; whatever empathetic problems Maia's wedding had knocked loose had also greased faerie abilities I used to have to strain for.

But the tendril just lay there, limp, at my feet. It didn't snake out toward anything like it should have—not out toward the dance floor, and not out toward the bar.

Lily was gone.

CHAPTER TWENTY-FOUR

I threw the spell out again as soon as I was back on the street. This time, the glowing green vine uncurled and stretched out down the street, sprouting leaves as it grew. I followed it, reeling the magic back into my aura as I went.

She was headed south, no doubt off to catch a bus that would take her to Oregon City and Evan. But the magic slithered past the first bus stop I passed and headed in a straight line down the road.

I was halfway through a crosswalk before I saw the car coming at me. I dodged forward, out of the way, just as it slammed on its brakes and jolted to a stop. The window rolled down.

"Are you okay?" the driver called.

Only in Portland, pedestrian capital of the universe, would he be looking at me with that kind of concern.

"I am so sorry," I said.

I glanced up. His light had been green, and my crosswalk had been labeled with a giant red hand saying DON'T WALK.

"That was totally my fault."

"But are you okay?"

"I'm fine," I said. "Thank you so much. I'm sorry."

He waved, and I turned and crashed into someone.

One crisis after another. It was a metaphor for my day.

She held me out at arm's length.

"I'm so sorry," she said. "I was trying to catch you."

I backed up and saw Amani looking down at me, her wildly curling hair adorned with glimmering raindrops. I glanced over my shoulder, somehow feeling like the Oracle was watching us. She probably was. There was water everywhere.

"I realized it would be faster to find you than to wait at the bus stop," Amani said.

"I have to catch my client," I said.

"Let's walk and talk," she said.

She held up a hand and rubbed her fingers rapidly together like she was trying to snap and was terrible at it. Her magic settled over my skin like cobwebs. I pulled my glasses down and saw a thick white haze surrounding us, thousands of tiny strands of magic woven together into that same thick fabric she'd used at the magic shop. This was a spell that didn't let anything in or out.

My spell snaked on ahead, but it wasn't connected to me anymore. Instead, it attached itself to the light bubble and pulled us along.

"Is this safe?" I said. "From the Oracle, I mean. Will this hide us from her?"

Amani looked sharply at me. "Yes," she said.

"Good." I took a deep breath.

This was the most audacious, crazy thing I'd ever done. No one in their right minds would accuse the Oracle of something like this, especially to the Faerie Queen.

But I trusted Amani. I had to trust her. If I was right, she'd know. If I was wrong… I'd cross that bridge when I came to it.

The words tumbled out of my mouth as fast as I could form them. She listened as we walked, her mouth drawn into a tight line. I couldn't tell if she was upset or not, but I kept talking, forcing myself to remember everything Lily had said.

"She talked like it was a game," I said. "Like Glim kids started it and then the Oracle started supporting it." I could hear my voice getting too high and too fast. "I know how crazy this sounds."

"It's not crazy," Amani said in a low voice.

Startled, I looked up. Her face had hardened into a mask.

She stopped walking and stared forward into the empty street, then closed her eyes and took in a long, deep breath.

It didn't seem to help. Her shoulders looked as tight and hard as a stone statue's.

"Are you okay?" I asked.

She winced as though I'd punched her. I could feel the panic and fear boiling up inside her. She took another deep breath in, fighting to control it.

A familiar silver shield began shimmering at the edges of our bubble, and vines began to uncurl around us. Amani watched them grow and then, with a long sigh, the bubble faded back to white.

"I'm so sorry," she said. "I, uh…"

She trailed off and looked down at me, her eyes searching as if I had the words she needed.

"I know you work closely with the Oracle," I said. "This must make your job a lot harder."

"It's more than that," she said.

I could see her evaluating me, trying to decide how much she could say. And then, her defenses seemed to crumble. Her shoulders relaxed and her entire face seemed to soften, not in a gentle way but as if she didn't have the strength to keep herself together.

"I wanted to be wrong," she said.

"You knew?" I said, but she winced, and I moved to the more important question. "What do we do now? Can the Oracle just be replaced?"

Could Amani do that? What would happen to the city?

"The Oracle is like the Faerie Queen," Amani said, her gaze distant and glazed. "The Glimmers change but the job stays the same."

"So can you deal with her? Are you—"

Was she strong enough? I didn't know how to ask that.

"I don't know," Amani said. "Um, I don't think so. It's not just the job, it's—Kelda and I have a lot of history."

It was my turn to search her face, and I felt almost burned by what I saw. Amani was hurt and she was afraid. And I understood her, because I was afraid, too.

"Kelda," I said.

"The Oracle." Amani fidgeted, tapping her fingernails against her palm in a frantic rhythm. "We grew up together. We've always had different ideas of the way things should be done."

Questions burned on my tongue. I pressed it to the roof of my mouth to keep myself silent.

Amani squeezed her hands into fists and seemed to steel herself. She looked down at me again, and this time, she seemed to see me.

"We need to keep going," she said. We began moving again, following the spell. My gaze focused as the vine's tip turned right and disappeared around a brick corner.

I held out a hand and the vine stopped dead, then shriveled and crumbled to dust as I let go of my hold. The magic dissipated in the air. It had been a small spell, but I felt its absence. It left an emptiness behind, a drained feeling like being tired.

My aura would fill back up. Quickly, if the runoff from Queen Amani's crackling magic had anything to do with it.

"Lily's not going to find Evan," I said.

My heart threw itself against my ribcage. I heard Lily's voice in my head: *Does the Oracle really grant wishes?*

Amani was already ahead of me.

"I heard this was a difficult case," she said.

I didn't bother to ask how she knew. She'd been watching me.

Everyone had been watching me.

"What should I do?"

"Normally I'd say it's up to your professional judgment," Amani said. "But I need your help."

"You have it," I said.

A wild look had lit in her eyes, a mad faerie gleam I hadn't seen there before. I dared myself to reach out a hand and touch her arm.

"Your Majesty," I said, suddenly understanding that she needed to know this. "You always have my help."

She looked down at me, and surprise mingled with her fire.

"I need you to go watch," she said. "Take the ring. Go find your client. And just watch. See what happens. I can't do anything; she's so elusive and I can't prove anything with her sprites protecting her. This could be bad, Olivia. I don't want a war."

"No one wants a war," I said.

I pulled my ring out and slipped it off its chain. It settled snug on my finger.

"She wants a war," Amani said. She grabbed my shoulders. "Be careful."

It was almost midnight. The Oracle would spring into being when the clock struck twelve.

Amani ripped open a hole in the fabric for me to escape through, and I ran.

Water fell from the Oracle's Fountain in sheets that rippled black and silver in the night. The street was quiet, the road deserted. The sidewalk glistened from the rain.

From the sidewalk, as far from the Fountain as I could be without stumbling backward into the road, I watched.

Lily stood at the bottom of the wide steps that led down to the Fountain. She had her arms wrapped around her body against the cold and the darkness.

It was ten minutes to midnight.

My phone buzzed in my pocket, briefly interrupting the sound of rushing water. My heart skipped a beat and Lily turned, her red hair shifting like a patchwork cloak behind her.

"Olivia!" she said. Her voice was too bright. She knew she'd be in trouble.

I waved her off. Blood pounded through my body, making my arms throb and my chest ache, but I had to be casual. I walked down the steps. Every step closer to the Fountain made my body feel tighter, but I forced my attention onto my client.

"I thought you ran off to find Evan," I said.

"I did better than that," she said.

Even in the darkness beneath the trees, we stood close enough that the joy on her face was impossible to miss. She clasped her hands together in front of her chest.

"If I go see Evan tonight, I'll have to keep seeing him until I convince him to marry me. But with the Oracle's help, all our problems will be solved. I can't believe we didn't think of it earlier!"

"Wow," I said.

Lily couldn't tell the difference between real and sarcastic enthusiasm and beamed at me.

"I asked him to meet me here in half an hour," she said.

I took a step forward. The Fountain's water rippled ominously in the dark.

"Asked him how?"

She pulled a small flip phone out of her pocket. Its front screen flashed on, vivid white and painfully bright.

"I got this from Goose House," she said. "I'm sorry I didn't tell you, but I suspected you would try to take it away from me. It's a… what's it called… pay-as-you-go. I help in the kitchens and they pay for my phone. Everyone in my Land Life Communications class got one." She looked down and added absently, "I'm learning to text."

Her eyes shone in the light of the phone, and they seemed bigger than usual.

I bit the inside of my cheek and tried to count slowly to ten. I got as far as seven before blurting, "Lily, you have an appointment to see him soon. And we've been talking about how you're not supposed to contact him on your own for months. Literally months. This is not a good idea."

I glanced at the Fountain. The Oracle hadn't emerged yet; even so, I could practically feel her eyes on me.

But Lily's attention was glued to the phone's glowing screen.

"He agrees with you," she said. Her voice came out flat and suddenly devoid of its love-crazed sparkle. "He said his fiancée doesn't like us seeing each other. I don't know why he told her about me."

"Because he's a good human being?" I said.

She wasn't listening. Her fingers flew across the little keyboard and she hunched down against the breeze.

"I'll tell him it's an emergency," she muttered.

"Lily," I said, but she whirled on me.

"You have to make him love me!" she cried.

When I didn't instantly agree, she turned back around to face the Fountain. She rocked back and forth on the balls of her feet like she'd had legs to fidget with all her life.

Tiny droplets of rain prickled against my face. I pulled out my own phone. Six minutes to go, and I had two texts, one from earlier in the evening and one from just now.

Lucas: Did you get a chance to talk to Imogen?

Lucas: She's acting really weird.

I threw a tiny invisible bubble around my hands to protect my phone from the rain and texted back while I typed. Lily stared resolutely at the Fountain in front of us.

Olivia: We talked at her sister's wedding. She has problems. But she's not my problem.

Four minutes to go.

Lucas: What happened between you two?

I didn't have time for this. Imogen was a tiny drop in the ocean of my problems right this second. I went for honesty.

Olivia: You happened. Imogen knew I liked you, and she lied to me and started dating you without talking to me first. And I'm happy you're both happy, but I don't need someone in my life who treats me like that.

I shoved the phone back in my pocket, and the Fountain erupted.

CHAPTER TWENTY-FIVE

I'd seen it before, but I still stumbled back as the water burst into the sky in shimmering silver geysers. The Oracle's face flickered behind a curtain of water and her voice filled my mind.

"Lily Pacifica," the Oracle boomed.

Lily trembled on her feet. In spite of myself, I reached out a hand to steady her. She sank into a low curtsy.

"Your Sorcerousness," she said.

"Your Honor," I whispered.

"Your Honor," Lily repeated, but the Oracle spoke over her.

"You have come on an errand of true love," she said.

"Yes, Your Honor," Lily said.

She was over her awe at once, rapture replacing her nerves and filling her eyes with light.

"He is my soulmate, the only one who can ever make me happy," she said.

The Oracle's pale face rippled behind the softly falling water. "Your parents disapprove."

"Yes, Your Honor," Lily said. "I don't care."

"You would choose this human over your inheritance?" the Oracle said, as if anyone had to ask.

"Oh, yes," Lily said. "He is all I want, Oracle. Please." Lily glanced sidelong at me and offered a tiny apologetic smile before saying, "My faerie godmother has tried her hardest, and I appreciate her efforts, I truly do. But Oracle, I can't bear another day without him. Please, grant my wish."

"And what is your wish?" the Oracle said.

I twisted the ring on my finger, feeling for the mirror, making sure it faced the Fountain. I held my breath and silently willed Lily to not say what I knew she was about to say.

She stepped forward until her new legs teetered on the edge of the Fountain's pool. Her whole body thrummed with yearning.

"I wish," she said, her voice clear and resolute. "I wish for Evan Costner to fall madly in love with me, tonight. For him to recognize that I am the only woman he could ever love, and to take me into his heart and his life with no hesitation or reservation. I have given up my world for him. I want him to give up his for me."

The words, romantic on the surface, turned my stomach over. But I forced my traitorous faerie features to behave. I was here to be the calm, supportive godmother, letting her client make her own choices while still guiding her Story with a careful hand.

My job was to do, not to judge.

The Oracle's water sparkled as threads of silver magic fell through the flickering curtain of water. The Oracle's spells were strong enough that even elf glass couldn't shield me.

"Step into the Fountain," the Oracle ordered.

Lily obeyed at once. She slipped out of her shoes and into the dark pool as though those steps were the only ones she had ever been destined to take. Her pale white feet shimmered beneath the surface as clear water lapped around her ankles.

The silver threads swam for her like fish attacking prey. They latched on to her, wrapped around her ankles and slithered up her body beneath her skirt to emerge from the neck and sleeves of her shirt. The lines glinted as they wrapped around her arms and snaked across her enraptured face.

I flinched and closed my eyes against the sudden blaze. White light shone from each thread as if each silver surface reflected pure moonlight.

And then the light faded, and the threads were gone, melted into Lily's own network of veins as they pulsed silently beneath her skin.

She let out a deep sigh. Her eyelids fell closed, and I reached out a hand to steady her. But she didn't sway. She stood for a moment, then stretched out her arms as if getting used to her body for the first time.

And then she stepped back out of the pool. A dark puddle dripped onto the cement. She bowed low.

"Thank you, Your Honor," she said.

"May you live happily ever after," the Oracle said, and then her white face shifted slightly and turned to me. "I wish to speak with your godmother."

"Of course," Lily said.

She bowed again and stepped back. She looked behind us, down the street, but Evan wasn't there yet. He would get lost and be unable to find our block, or get distracted, or accidentally miss his turn. He was a Humdrum; he wouldn't be able to find us until the Oracle was gone.

I felt for the ring with my thumb. The mirror still faced outward.

The hairs on my arms stood up. The Oracle had always intimidated me, but she had never frightened me. Not till now. I shielded my emotions instantly, directing them all toward Lily and my case.

"Thank you, Your Honor," I said. I stepped forward. "I hadn't intended to resolve the case this way, but now I see we should have come to you in the first place."

"You did well enough," the Oracle said. "But we have more important things to discuss."

The ring burned hot on my finger. I focused my attention onto Lily and how angry I was with her. That was a safe thing to think about. That was the only safe thing right now.

"Times are changing," the Oracle said. "Our community is growing. There are more Glimmers in this city than there were when you were born. Indeed, there are more Glimmers in this city than there were yesterday."

There was nothing to say to that, so I waited. But she waited, too. The silence stretched out until I shifted and said, "My dad says our population is growing."

"And how is your father?" the Oracle asked. "He is a fine leader in our community."

This hadn't been the line of questioning I expected. I shrugged.

"He's having some trouble at work," I said.

The moment the words came out, I regretted them. My dad's job was a problem because he hadn't been able to catch the person targeting the Humdrums. That person was right in front of me. It wasn't a conversation I wanted to bring up.

"I'm aware of his difficulties," she said. "Do you know why he's having such trouble?"

"Not really," I lied. "I just know he's under a lot of stress."

And he took it out on us, and it was all thanks to her. I filed that thought away; I couldn't follow it through to any kind of conclusion without letting my emotions leak out to where the water rippled in the light of the street lamps.

"Your father is attempting to protect the Humdrums from Glimmers who wish to see them gone," the Oracle said. "The Humdrums are being attacked in increasing numbers, and your father wishes to shield them. But it's a losing battle."

"Who wants to see them gone?" I said, hoping her confession might make a difference. "What makes it a losing battle?"

"I had hoped a faerie of your caliber would go deeper," the Oracle said. "The question, Olivia Feye, is *why*."

"Why *what?*" I said. There were too many possible questions, and I was pretty sure I'd asked some of them already. "Why is my dad trying to protect them? Or why are they being attacked in the first place?"

"That's the one," the Oracle said. Her voice was warm with approval. It sent prickles down my spine.

I heard Lily's footsteps behind me. I didn't know if she could hear this conversation, but I was almost grateful to her for standing there, keeping me from being alone with the Oracle.

"There is a storm brewing," the Oracle continued. "We Glimmers need space to grow and breathe."

"So someone's getting the Humdrums out of the way," I said.

The *someone* felt huge in my mouth, and I wondered if she could see through my feigned ignorance to my fluttering heartbeat.

"Glimmers are superior," the Oracle said. "A superior organism's needs must take precedence. Even you must understand that."

It was hard to see her expressions; all I could tell was that she was pale, with dark eyes, and that she stared at me as intensely as I stared back at her.

"My dad's mentioned things," I said. "Hauntings."

"They cannot be scared by anything they do not already fear," the Oracle said. "These attacks on the Humdrums—what are they? Have they been harmed? No. They run from their own fear. Their run from their own legends, their own ghost stories. They fear us, and so they flee."

I rubbed my arms briskly as a night breeze crept down the collar of my jacket. Spray kicked up from the Fountain and misted cold across my face.

"Fear is their enemy," she said. "Courage must be our ally. We must cease fearing who we are, and who we may become. If allowed to flourish, who can tell what greatness we may achieve? But no Glim can grow in a field choked with weeds. Only when there is room to breathe will we reach our full potential. Do you understand, Olivia Feye?"

I felt my tongue move, warm and damp in my mouth, but my jaw seemed frozen. *Pull it together, Feye,* I ordered.

I was Olivia Feye. The Faerie Queen had chosen me to be here, for this conversation, in this moment. I could do this.

"I think I understand," I said. I forced my mouth to stay open, to keep talking. "You want the Humdrums gone. You think we'll be better off without them."

The air around the Fountain seemed to disperse, as though the water itself had let out a great sigh.

"The Faerie Queen has approached you, I believe," she said.

I clenched the hand with the ring on it. I hadn't told anyone about that. Queen Amani had said she wouldn't tell anyone, either. Even the Oracle shouldn't know about something the Faerie Queen had promised to keep quiet.

But of course, she'd been watching.

I was so tired of being watched.

"The Glimmering world is changing," the Oracle said. "It changes every day, more and more quickly. And it needs you, for you can alter the tides."

I squinted at the fountain. She spoke in riddles—great magical beings usually did—but this was the first time I had ever felt truly, genuinely like I didn't have a clue what she was talking about.

"You will not have noticed your importance, no doubt," she said. "Your eyes are turned away from our world, toward your commonplace goals of school and career. You do not sense there could be something more. This is not surprising. Many of the greatest Glimmers have been unable to use their gifts for themselves. But it is time to pay attention, Olivia. It is time to see your potential."

Suddenly, and for reasons totally unrelated to the late hour and the danger of prying into the Oracle's affairs, I wished I hadn't come. My stomach tied itself into a sinking knot I couldn't interpret.

"Queen Amani has extended the role of the next Faerie Queen to you," the Oracle said, and it wasn't a question. "I have seen this much through divination. She shows her wisdom in this. But I also desire you at my side."

"This is *wrong*." The words burst out of me, loud enough to interrupt, loud enough to cut off the crazy, overwhelming thing she was saying at the source.

But my reprieve lasted only a moment. The Oracle wasn't my parents or Imogen, and I couldn't talk over her voice in my head.

"War is coming," she said. "It is coming quickly. Glimmers will side with their own kind or with the Humdrums, but we must all choose a side. I want you on my side. You can lead this fight, Olivia. You can make our world blossom into the majesty fate has always intended."

My eyes were so wide I felt the breeze drying them out. I could imagine a bug flying into one at any second, just because it couldn't help running into anything so large. But I couldn't relax my eyelids. I couldn't blink even for a second.

"War seems super unnecessary," I said. "War is the first thing I would rule out if I were as important as you think I am."

Her voice thundered into my head. "Necessary or not, it is coming, and you will not escape," she said. "Make your choice. Someone else already has."

I stared at the Oracle as her white face rippled under its curtain. She met my eyes with her black hollow ones, and then her face shifted ever so slightly to look behind me. I spun around.

Imogen stood in the sharp yellow lamplight. Her eyes were water-dark and stared straight through me.

CHAPTER TWENTY-SIX

The Oracle's eyes fixed on me. She blinked, and her face slid back into the shadows, leaving behind only water rippling with darkness.

Lily, who had been distracted from her wait for Evan by Imogen's appearance, looked between Imogen and me and seemed to slink back. She held up her phone.

"Evan is almost here," she whispered. "He drove too far. I'll be back."

I heard her footsteps disappear down the sidewalk along the edge of the darkened park. And then it was just the two of us, staring across the empty ground at each other. The gentle burbling of the Fountain laced through the air around us.

"She chose you," Imogen said, her voice as dull as her eyes.

My feet moved me toward her before I could think about it.

"Imogen," I said. "Are you okay?"

She didn't blink, just stared at me with that blank expression.

"She chose *you*," Imogen said again, the slight inflection barely enough to make a dent in her flat monotone.

"So? I don't know what she's talking about," I said. I reached out a hand but didn't dare touch her. "Gen, what's wrong?"

"Not the Oracle," Imogen said. "The Faerie Queen. She chose you."

"Oh," I said. "Yeah."

We stared at each other for a long moment. Her jaw twitched, just once.

"What are you doing here?" I said.

"The Oracle called me," she said.

"Why?" I said.

She blinked, but she looked into the distance as though I might have not been there at all.

"Why did she call you?" I demanded.

She was silent a long moment, and then, with a wave of heat like someone had opened a furnace, her eyes snapped to mine, fully conscious and blazing. I jumped back as though I'd been burned.

"*Someone* had to choose me," she hissed.

I couldn't believe what I was hearing. Hot faerie anger rolled off her. I let it engulf me.

"People choose you all the time," I said.

"Lucas," she said, and the name tossed off her tongue like it meant nothing. "Yeah, great. I get the Humdrum boy. You get our kingdom."

Her jaw twitched again. I saw her hands in my peripheral vision, clenched into white fists at her sides.

I couldn't believe what I was hearing.

"Are you going to hit me?" I said. "Just because someone picked me over you for once in our lives?"

Imogen Dann had the spoiled little rich girl act down to a science.

"You're lucky if I don't," she said.

"I don't care if you do," I said.

I felt my own anger rise off my skin like scalding steam. Her magic sparked gold outside the frame of my glasses. It sputtered and showered down on us with a feeling like hot pinpricks.

"The world isn't about you, Imogen."

"You've made that perfectly clear," she said.

"I've made that clear? *I've* made that clear?"

I could hear my voice growing shrill, but I couldn't stop it. I wanted to scream into her face just to make her hear me. Suddenly, it didn't matter that the Oracle was watching.

"I have lived in your shadow since we were nine," I said. "When Queen Amani asked me, I said no, because I've had the spotlight so rarely that I don't even know what to do with it. And I'm the one with the problem?"

"I don't care about the Faerie Queen," Imogen said.

A laugh barked up from my throat. She was about to knock me over with the worst spell in her arsenal, judging from the way the magic gathered around her. I brought my hands up and threw out a pulsing white shield. It was only visible outside my glasses, leaving the center of my vision as two dark rectangles framing Imogen's flushed face.

"You just care that she didn't see how special and magical and sparkly you are first," I said.

Imogen's lip trembled, her fury turning her face into a mask with hot red cheeks.

"You lied to me," she said.

"Now you know how it feels," I said.

"You lied to me *first*," she said.

I opened my mouth to tell her she was crazy and needed to get off her damn high horse. And then I remembered.

She was right.

I'd forgotten.

I silently counted back how many months it had been in my head. With each number, my stomach got a little heavier until I couldn't quite breathe.

The shield around my body rippled and dispersed, the white membrane pulling apart and dissolving into nothing.

"You lied to me," Imogen whispered.

"I—"

"I thought you were being weird," she interrupted. "And I thought it was just your parents freaking you out. And then everything happened with Lucas and it was way too fast." She took a step toward me. "You *know* how I am with guys, Olivia." As if it was my fault, as if I should have seen her coming. "And I tried to tell you, I swear to Titania. But then you flipped out at me and I didn't know what to do. You wouldn't freaking text me. You've never been mad enough that you wouldn't text me."

Any reply I might have made was a ball in my throat.

Had I really not told her?

I remembered thinking that it was complicated, and that Amani had asked for privacy.

"She told me not to tell anyone," I said, but my voice was even weaker than my words.

Yes, Amani had asked for secrecy. But now, staring at Imogen, it hit me as if all the cold water from the Oracle's Fountain was crashing over my head at once: She hadn't meant *this*. I could have at least asked.

I cleared my throat and tried again. The words struggled to get out.

"I didn't want you to be disappointed in me for saying no," I said.

For some reason, this truth was harder to admit than the comfortable excuses I'd given myself for months. Everyone was always disappointed in me. Adding Imogen to that list would have made me worse than nothing.

"And then the Oracle told me," Imogen said, like I hadn't spoken. "I wanted to talk to her about you, because I knew I'd been stupid about Lucas, but you wouldn't even let me apologize." She scoffed. "Not that an apology would have done any good. You're going to run off to that stupid Humdrum college no matter what I do."

"What does that have to do with anything?"

"You really think we would have survived that?"

I stared at Imogen, waiting for her to make some sense, but her face was as cold and white as marble.

"You hate Glims," she said. "You've always wanted friends like Lucas, friends who don't remind you of our world. Your stupid college would have been full of them. But I still tried, Olivia. I still went to the Oracle to see if maybe she thought our friendship could be saved. You are the one person who is important enough that I would bother the goddamned freaking *Oracle* over you not talking to me."

Her words sounded almost as strangled as mine. And while her face seemed still and under control, I saw her jaw twitch, and I saw her eyes flinch. She could pretend not to feel it, but I knew her better than that.

I knew *us* better than that.

"I tried to talk to you," I said.

"Yeah," she said. "At my sister's wedding, which you were *not* there for, which you did *not* help me with. You knew how stressed out I was about that wedding, Olivia. You knew that. And so you just skipped all the time leading up to it and showed up in time for cake."

"I came to apologize," I said.

"Why should I have let you apologize?" she said. "I'd been trying to tell you I was sorry for months."

"I was upset."

Her words cut over me. "I went to the Oracle to ask about you," she said. "And she said you were probably just stressed because of Queen Amani. And I asked her what she was talking about, and she said she'd assumed you'd told me. Even the Oracle made that mistake. Even the Oracle assumed you would *tell* me about something like that."

Neither of us could keep the tears from rising. We stood there staring at each other like a couple of weepy babies, and I fought the water back into my eyes.

The Oracle, Lily the ocean princess, Queen Amani's palace hidden behind Oregon's tallest waterfall—there was too much water everywhere, too many glimmering waves threatening to crash over me. I fought to breathe. But there was no breathing, and there was no thinking straight. There was just me, messing up.

All these months, I'd been thinking about Imogen—how Imogen had stolen Lucas, how Imogen had turned on me, how Imogen had betrayed me and spilled my secrets and done everything she could to hurt me.

But I hadn't thought about me, not once. I'd thought about my feelings, and about all the ways Imogen had ruined my life, but I had pinned all the blame on her.

And that wasn't fair. We weren't standing here, staring at each other through the darkness, just because of her.

I could see it now, in the tightness in her shoulders and the shaking of my hands. It had been both of us. We'd taken turns making the wrong choices. Each of us had taken steps forward to meet in this moment.

"I'm so sorry," I said.

She watched me, her face as pale and blank as the Oracle's. Even so, she had to be hurting just as much as I was.

Any why not? I hadn't trusted her enough to tell her about Amani. I had been too afraid and too cowardly to risk her disappointment, and so I had shut her out of my life and hurt her just as much as she'd hurt me by not telling me she had feelings for Lucas.

She'd been wrong about that, but it wasn't all on her. I could have talked to him. Even after they started dating, I could have at least told him how I felt. Nothing had stopped me but me.

I could have responded to just one of Imogen's texts and let her sneak an apology in under all my anger. I could have given her one conversation—one interaction that would have been long enough to show me that she wasn't all right, that something was deeply and desperately wrong inside her.

I could have been there for her.

Maybe I could have even stopped us from breaking.

And maybe I could have stopped her from coming here, to make whatever decision she was going to make.

Beside us, the Fountain loomed, dark and threatening.

I bit the inside of my cheek. The pain gave me something to focus on, and I forced myself to take a big enough breath to squeeze out the words.

"Gen, I'm sorry," I repeated. "I was wrong. We both were."

Imogen looked up at the trees shifting darkly above us, then swallowed and looked back down at me.

"I don't care," she said.

I wrestled with my face, trying to keep it from crumpling. And then my head jerked up, and Imogen's snapped to the side, because there were footsteps running toward us. I bit hard on the inside of my cheek and waited for whatever Glimmer was running to catch the Oracle while she was still awake for midnight. Let them have the Oracle and her horrible advice. I was done.

But it wasn't a Glimmer. It was someone who shouldn't have been there at all.

Lucas jogged into sight, his hair flopping and his figure looking even lankier than usual as he ran. He saw us and ran down the steps, relief all over his face.

"I'm so glad I found you," he gasped. He grabbed Imogen by the shoulders. "What do you mean, *Have a good life?*"

She wouldn't meet his eyes. Her face looked too skinny. I wondered if she'd been eating. She dieted too much when she was stressed.

"I meant it," Imogen said. Her gaze flickered to me for the briefest second before landing back on him. "You're a good guy. You deserve to have a good life."

"What do you think you're going to do?" he said. "You're scaring me."

"I'm not suicidal," she said, voice dull again. "I'm just done."

"Done with what?"

I edged away. This felt too private.

"Done," she said. "With us, with you, with school, with my 'normal' life.. You can have normal." She looked suddenly up at him, her gaze hot again. "I'm finished."

Lucas pulled her close, crushing her in a hug that she didn't return.

"Don't be done," he said, and he sounded way too vulnerable and upset. I wanted to comfort him but knew that would only make it worse. I stepped back again.

He looked over at me. An edge of confusion entered and then left his expression.

"Hi, Olivia," he said.

I nodded. I didn't trust myself to speak.

He turned back to Imogen. "What's going on?" he said. "Come on. You can talk to me."

She laughed, totally without humor. "I can *not* talk to you," she said. "Good Titania, the levels on which I cannot talk to you make my head spin."

His eyebrows drew up as though they were trying to recoil and protect themselves. He held her at arm's length and tried to look into her evasive eyes.

"Could you maybe just try?"

"No," she said loudly, staring at him as though trying to explain something to a slow toddler. "It's illegal for me to talk to you, Lucas."

"How are you here?" I said.

The Oracle's Fountain was alive. No Humdrum should have been able to step onto this block.

He shrugged one shoulder. "I drove," he said. "My mom's car."

It wasn't what I'd meant, but I couldn't explain what I'd meant. Especially not in front of the Oracle. Imogen was right. It was all kinds of not permitted. I ran a hand all over my face. Tension dispersed and tingled all across my skin.

Imogen carefully, firmly, pulled Lucas' hands off her shoulders.

"But you know what?" she said. "Screw it. Screw all the secrets."

She dropped his hands to his sides and turned back to me. She stared at me, eyes harsh in the darkness, and opened her mouth. But she couldn't seem find anything to say, because I wasn't worth the effort. She closed it again and shook her head as if she could brush me off like an annoying fly.

She straightened her shoulders and walked toward the Oracle's Fountain, where the water rippled quiet and black.

"I'm ready," she announced.

I didn't even have time to yell before the black curtain parted. Instead of revealing the Oracle's face, it opened onto a long dark tunnel that disappeared into the heart of the Fountain.

I couldn't move quickly enough. Before I could force my feet to move, or even force my mind to realize what was happening, Imogen had stepped into the pool. She turned to look over her shoulder. Our eyes met for a long, silent second. Her blush-blond hair glinted in the soft reaches of the streetlamp and her eyes flashed their reflection.

And then she was gone.

I ran forward, hand outstretched, as the water closed over her with a roar.

The scream that hadn't been able to claw its way up my throat finally erupted into the night. I threw myself into the Fountain and clawed at the place she'd disappeared. Solid stone met my hand behind the icy curtain.

CHAPTER TWENTY-SEVEN

I didn't know how long it was before I felt Lucas' arms pulling me back. He wrapped his arms firmly around my shoulders, and I let him steer me away from the rush of water and back over the lip of the pool.

I was soaked through. My body shivered like it was strapped to a jackhammer, but I wasn't cold. I couldn't feel anything but a deep panic that felt like it was here to stay, like one long scream that went on forever.

"She's gone," I said. "Lucas, she's gone."

The Fountain roared to life with another enormous spray of white water.

"Whoa!" Lucas shouted.

I heard his feet stumble backward on the pavement, but I held my ground. The Oracle's face appeared as the white water fell into the pools with an echoing splash.

I marched toward her.

"Where is she?" I demanded.

"Imogen is safe with me," she said.

Her voice was too calm. Fury rose up, prickling the hair on my arms and making the hair on my head feel as though it were about to catch fire.

"Where is she?" I repeated, as though the almighty Oracle was too stupid to understand the first time.

I had spent my whole life fearing and respecting this being. Now, I wanted to reach through the water again and hit her shimmering pale face until it cracked like porcelain.

I felt my hands knot into fists. "Why did you tell her?"

The Oracle's face didn't move, but it seemed to take on a sinister expression, not something I could see but instead an energy radiating from the Fountain and into my bones.

"Why didn't you?"

"That is none of your business," I said, and while part of me couldn't believe my audacity, the other part of me wanted to take the world's largest flame torch to the Fountain until it disappeared and left her with nowhere to go and nothing to hide behind.

Too late, I remembered the ring on my finger. Amani had seen it all. And, I realized, I didn't care. This wasn't Amani's business, either.

"What did you do to her?" I said.

"Imogen has declared her allegiance to me," the Oracle said. "You will see her again. In the meantime, I advise you to appreciate your friend's wisdom and choose your side accordingly. I can change your world, Olivia Feye. I can give you Imogen back. I can make Lucas love you. These things are child's play for the people who are wise enough to follow me."

I opened my mouth to shout at her, but her voice cut into my head.

"We will speak again."

And then her face was gone, and the looming sense of dread emanating from the Fountain was gone, and the streetlights seemed brighter, and Lucas was breathing hard behind me.

I waited, half-expecting her to erupt again with some new and thrilling way to ruin my life. A scream rose up in my throat. I choked it back and waited.

The park stayed still. A car drove past the fountain.

A long silence hung between us, snaking through the tree branches and flooding the ground on which we stood. I couldn't speak. Lucas couldn't speak, but a blend of fear and confusion slipped up and down his veins with his blood. Every heartbeat held the questions *what* and *why.* I felt every last one of his breaths, and I stared hard at the nearest streetlamp to focus my energy on it and push him out.

Before I could manage it, he spoke. "What just happened?"

There was no way to explain. I couldn't even begin.

And then other people crept into my awareness, an excited presence and a vaguely familiar one I couldn't quite place.

Lily skipped around the edge of the Fountain, her footsteps as light as if she was dancing. She had cut through the park, and she dragged Evan along by the hand. He followed as though he wasn't even aware he was doing it.

I hadn't gotten much of an impression from him when we'd first met, and I didn't get much of an impression now. The enchantment that dripped from him, though, was strong enough to knock me over. His glazed eyes had trouble focusing on me, and he couldn't seem to tell exactly where his feet were.

"Faerie godmother!" Lily cried.

The pure glee in her voice made my stomach twist in knots. She ran toward me, Evan jogging awkwardly behind. She let go of his hand to throw her arms around my neck.

"We did it," she whispered into my ear. "Thank you!"

I pulled her off me, my eyes searching hers.

"Did what?" I demanded.

"Evan and I are together!" she said, as though this was the greatest announcement anyone had ever made. "We're in love!"

"I'm in love with her," Evan repeated, looking too seriously at me.

"You're in love with your fiancée," I said firmly.

"I'm in love with Lily," he said.

My hands flew to my temples. I didn't have enough hands to hold myself together. My seams were unraveling.

Lily's face glowed. My stomach turned over.

"The Oracle granted my wish!" she said. "She knew it was all right for all my dreams to come true! And now they have!"

"What is happening?" Lucas said. We all ignored him, me because I could only handle one crisis at a time, Lily because she was a self-centered monster, and Evan because he was clearly stoned out of his mind by some enchantment.

"After we spoke, she appeared to me in the park," Lily said. "And oh, faerie godmother, she's lovely, and she wants me to be so happy! She wants Evan and me to get married, and he can take photographs and I can paint and sculpt and together we'll be the most perfect couple! So we made a bargain."

I grabbed onto her arm. It wasn't quite enough to keep me steady.

"I know," I said. "I was there. She granted your wish."

"She's done so much more than that," Lily said.

An undercurrent of warmth swept through her voice, an almost religious fervor that made nerves prickle up my spine.

"She knew one wish wouldn't be enough to guarantee a lifetime of love," she said. "And she wants Evan and me to be in love forever. But a spell like that needs such incredible magic. So I promised to give her my voice—my allegiance and support for when she tries to save the Glimmering world, and the allegiance of all the mermaids I can convince—and in return, she wove an enchantment that binds him to me forever!"

"I love her," Evan said.

I wanted to slap him awake. He'd at least been pleasant and alive when we'd met. The man in front of me was a glassy-eyed puppet. And Lily didn't even notice.

"You couldn't make him love me, but she did, and oh, faerie godmother, we're going to be so happy!" she said. "Thank you for telling me about her!"

How was it possible for so many things to go wrong so quickly? I'd come here to alert Queen Amani to a potential hot tip. I hadn't meant for the world to fall apart.

I needed to be alone.

"You should probably go have your happily ever after," I said.

I couldn't believe how flat my voice sounded. I couldn't believe I managed to have a voice at all.

"We could get champagne," Evan said, way more earnestly than any beverage could justify.

"Oh, darling!" Lily cried.

She tried to hug me again, but I stopped her.

"Go," I said. "Now."

She was too excited to notice that her arms hadn't managed to fling around my neck.

"Thank you, faerie godmother!" she said.

She turned to Evan and kissed him, the kind of deep, intense kiss that should have meant the movie ended well.

They ran off into the night together, Lily laughing and Evan repeating "I love you! You're beautiful! I love you!" over and over, like an obnoxious talking doll that only knew two phrases.

I'd been holding my breath without realizing it. I let the air escape on a long, tired sigh that wanted to take my whole body with it. I wanted to crumple to a heap on the ground and pass out for a hundred years like a good old-fashioned Sleeping Beauty.

Instead, I turned to Lucas. His shoulders and legs were tense, ready to run.

How was I supposed to break this kind of news to a Humdrum? I'd spent my whole life wishing I was one of them. I'd never once thought about what I would say if I ever had to tell one of them about us.

In the end, I didn't have to. He ran a hand across his lips and chin as though smoothing an imaginary beard and blurted, "You're magic."

Two words, I thought, with a surprised part of my brain that didn't seem to realize how much crap had just happened. Two words covered it.

I nodded, keeping a close eye on his face. He breathed in and out, slowly, as though worried he'd startle himself if he wasn't careful.

"That fountain has a… sorceress in it."

"A faerie," I said.

"Right," he said. "And you're—"

"A faerie."

"You're both faeries."

"That would be correct," I said.

"That would be hard to digest," he said.

"That would be why I never mentioned it," I said.

We stared at each other for another long moment.

My skin tingled. The only thing I wanted was to sit down somewhere far away from here, but I couldn't collect the pieces of my mind enough to figure out how to make it happen.

"And you like me," he said. "You and Imogen fought about it."

"I liked you," I corrected. "And yes. We're both idiots. She's a bigger idiot," I added, jerking my head toward the Fountain, which rippled innocently.

"Who is that thing?" he said. "That… faerie?"

"That's the Oracle," I said. "You're not supposed to be able to see her, but I guess she decided she just needed to complicate my life. Wouldn't be the first time."

I wanted to knock myself upside the head for coming here tonight. How had I thought that was a good idea? I'd spent my whole life fearing and honoring the Oracle. How had I underestimated her here, at last, when it finally mattered? How had Amani been crazy enough to think I could handle this?

"And she's evil?" he said.

"How'd you figure that one out?" I said.

The breeze prickled my skin into goosebumps, or maybe it was fear at saying something like that so close to the Fountain.

I had to get to Amani.

I felt for the silver ring. It was hot to the touch; I hoped that meant she was still watching.

I walked away toward the road, gesturing Lucas to follow me. I didn't look back.

Not until the now-familiar roar of spray hit my ears. I turned around to see the Fountain erupting back to life.

My blood stopped cold in my veins. Her eyes bored into me.

"And they lived happily ever after," she said.

Her voice sliced through my mind and sent pain reeling in spirals through my head and down my neck. She laughed, a giddy, manic sound, and then the spray of water fell and crashed to the pool with the weight of a thousand gold coins.

The coins poured from the Fountain and littered the rippling curtain with flashes of yellow. They filled the pool, cold metal pressing against cold metal until they looked like hundreds of tiny goldfishes struggling for room. Lucas' eyes were huge. I grabbed his arm.

"Run," I said.

For the first time that day, someone was smart enough to listen to me.

CHAPTER TWENTY-EIGHT

The next morning was a morning like any other.

It shouldn't have been.

The world should have ended. It should still be a darkened expanse filled with the clinking of gold coins. Instead, the sun shone out over trees whose leaves were just beginning to change. The ring on my finger stayed cool and quiet, though Amani's voice still echoed in my head: *Behave as though it's life as usual. I'll come find you soon.* Daniel and I had ignored each other over breakfast like always, and my classes had been quiet and uneventful, though I didn't remember any of them five minutes after.

I caught Lucas' eye in the hallway between Language Arts and U.S. History. He looked as distracted as I was, but we didn't get a chance to talk, and part of me was glad.

I couldn't stop the roaring of the Fountain in my ears.

When I got to work, the Oracle's Fountain stood quiet and bubbling, as it had every day since I'd begun working at Wishes Fulfilled. I gave it a wide berth.

On the top floor, my feet plodded down the too-thick runner carpet in the hall. I hovered just outside the doors of Wishes Fulfilled, unable to force myself in.

How was I supposed to justify what had happened to Lorinda? To Tabitha? To my parents, when, Titania forbid, they found out? I suddenly didn't have a client. And Lorinda always knew everything. She'd know I was somehow involved in the life-altering spell that had made Evan lose his mind, and worse, she'd know I was involved in a Humdrum being exposed to our world.

She caught sight of me in the open doorway and walked toward me in a pale pink suit.

"Olivia!" she boomed.

I cringed, waiting. But then she smiled, and her smile was huge.

How could anyone smile on a day like this? I couldn't think straight.

I held stiff and still while she squeezed my shoulders, her professional distance forbidding a hug but the excitement on her face making it impossible for her to stay away.

"Congratulations!" she said. "We are so proud of you!"

I let myself be patted on the back while my mind reeled.

Nothing made sense. I wished she'd stop talking so I could check my ring and see if Amani wanted to talk yet.

"Really well done, Olivia," Tabitha said, coming up behind Lorinda. She wore a little black dress covered in a slouchy cream shawl, looking as always like an elegant witch instead of pastel Lorinda's second-in-command. "I know that was a challenge for you, but you did what needed to be done. Good job."

I looked from one approving face to another. "What?" I said.

"Your case," Lorinda said. "The Oracle said you were unable to collect your gold yourself, so she had it delivered to the company account this morning. I transferred your portion to your bank."

"My what?" I repeated.

"Your bank," Lorinda said. She chuckled, as though my dimwittedness was delightful. "You'll find a healthy bonus there. The Oracle expressed her gratitude for your innovative thinking and felt you deserved a financial reward. I called your father to congratulate him and to find out if you were with Pacific Lunary Credit Union or Magpie Bank. We really need to get your direct deposit set up."

"You called my dad." I was a parrot, repeating words without having a clue what they meant.

She clapped a hand on my arm.

"I'm so sorry about that, dear. I assumed you'd told him already," she said. "He didn't have a clue what I was talking about, but I know he must be so proud of you!"

"I'm sure he is," I said. I blinked at her. "Wait. I thought you didn't want… that… to happen. Because of King Pacifica."

Tabitha edged in, her gentle voice a relief after Lorinda's.

"We think you worked it out brilliantly," she said. "The alliance you proposed between the Oracle and King Pacifica was accepted. It was a risky move, but I think you satisfied the Oracle *and* Neptune. I don't know why we didn't think of it sooner. Him stationing his sea nymphs in her fountains, her monitoring the land and protecting the tributaries that lead to the river—it's the perfect solution."

"And true love still gets to win in the end!" Lorinda said.

An ache crept up my jaw and into my head. Lorinda's emotions began to press in on me, an almost maternal pride that felt as suffocating as her hand on my shoulder.

I tolerated their congratulations for a few more minutes, until finally, the giant conch shell that served as Lorinda's Glimmering phone started blowing like a foghorn from her office. She bustled off.

Tabitha had been watching me a little too closely. She glanced to the copy machine, where Aster, one of the Junior Godmothers, was visibly eavesdropping.

"You okay?" she said.

I shrugged. "Sure."

"It must have been a busy week. Why don't you go find something really busy-looking to do in your cubicle?" she said. She nodded toward Lorinda's office. "She'll be a minute."

She didn't need to tell me twice.

I pulled up my bank account online. After Elle's case, I'd finally moved my money from a coin jar in my bedroom to Magpie Bank, and now I scanned my account for the latest transactions. I refreshed the page, convinced the number there was wrong.

The money was listed in gold coins. I wasn't sure exactly what the exchange rate to US dollars was these days, but the rough estimate in my head screamed loud and clear that I had enough to pay for college flat-out here if I kept myself on a budget. I stared at the deposit line, blinking and waiting for the numbers to fade away, or for a digit to drop off the end. But nothing on the screen moved except the flashing *Pythoness Apothecary: "Bewitching" supplies since 1937!* banner ad at the top of the page.

I was still staring when Lorinda found me again. She leaned into my cubicle.

"Phenomenal news!" she said. "Apparently Lily Pacifica has been trying to contact you all day but couldn't reach you."

I pulled my phone out of my pocket. Four texts were there, along with three missed calls. My phone was on vibrate, but I hadn't felt it go off once.

"She's officially engaged!" Lorinda trilled.

The sick feeling that had been with me since last night churned in my stomach. It was almost starting to feel normal.

"Evan proposed to her this morning down at the river by where they first met. And King Pacifica has given his full blessing to the union, though we've all agreed it's best not to let Evan know his bride's full history until they've known each other a bit longer."

"Because nothing says love like dishonesty," I said, finishing the words a split second before I realized they probably should have stayed in my head.

Lorinda's eyebrows drew together for a moment, but she looked more confused than upset.

"You've just done a fabulous job, Olivia," she said, brushing it off. "Really phenomenal. It's been a long time since we've had an intern who showed your kind of initiative and out-of-the-box thinking. Not only is your client happily engaged as the best possible ending to her Story, you also managed to create an alliance between two important Glimmering figures. I am so glad to have you on our team."

I had literally no idea what to say to any of that. I finally managed a smile and a "thanks," and then she was being interrupted by yet one more kink in my afternoon, this one in the form of Lucas coming up behind her, shadowed by a cautious Tabitha.

He was taller than both of them, but still managed to seem small and awkward next to Tabitha's alert gaze. Lorinda looked at him, opened her mouth, looked at me, looked back at him, and frowned.

"This gentleman is here to see you," Tabitha said.

She was behind Lucas and shot me a questioning look over his shoulder. *He's Humdrum,* she mouthed, her red lipstick framing the words in fire-engine urgency.

I closed the computer window and stood up. "What are you doing here?" I said.

"I thought I'd take you out to lunch," he said. His eyes darted toward Tabitha. "If that's okay."

What? Tabitha mouthed.

"Olivia," Lorinda said, a careful hint of caution in her voice.

"He's fine," I said.

"He's—" Lorinda started, then seemed unsure how to continue.

"He's a Humdrum," I said. "And I have no idea how he got here."

"Olivia?" Tabitha said.

I lowered my glasses and eyed him, trying to match his floppy dark hair and pleasant smile with any excuse for him to be here. But he was the only person in this room who didn't have magic rising from their skin.

"The Oracle has decided that Lucas is part of our world," I said. "I have no clue why."

"But," Lorinda said, then couldn't seem to figure out how to finish.

I folded my arms across my chest.

"But he's a Humdrum," I said. "I know. Through and through."

"I'm a what?" he said, one eyebrow quirking down.

"Humdrum," I said. A note of irritation crept into my tone that I couldn't figure out how to stifle. "It means you're not magical. Obviously."

He frowned at me, and I took a deep breath. *Focus on your breathing,* I ordered.

I counted out two breaths and then said, "Could Lucas and I have a minute, please?"

Lorinda looked between us, her curiosity making it hard for her to let it go, but they left. I had a feeling the other godparents were doing everything they could to listen in. Lucas shoved his hands into his pockets.

"So," he said. He rocked forward onto the balls of his feet. "You want to go get lunch?"

"I don't know," I said.

"Do you get a lunch?" he said. He flushed. The pale pink was gone as soon as it had appeared. "Sorry, I should have thought this out first. I should have texted you."

"Wouldn't have mattered," I said.

"Oh," he said. His face fell. "Okay. Yeah, that's cool."

"No," I said. "I mean I haven't been checking my phone today. I have a ton of missed messages. I wouldn't have seen yours."

"Oh," he said. Something in his expression seemed to lift again. "So, can you? Do you want to?"

"I don't know," I said again.

Why did people keep asking questions and saying things? I just wanted to sit alone where it was quiet and think.

"Or I could bring you something? We could eat here, maybe?"

He glanced around my little cubicle, his eyes taking in what little there was to see. If he'd been expecting something spectacular, the gray walls and five-year-old computer were guaranteed to disappoint.

He seemed sweet. And that was the problem.

"I'm a little confused about you," I said.

I couldn't tell where the balance between truth and politeness was, so I forged ahead and hoped it didn't matter.

"You're not supposed to know about me, and you kind of ruined the longest friendship of my life."

No, that was wrong.

I let out a big sigh.

"Correction: *I* ruined the longest friendship of my life," I said. "But you were involved. I know it's not your fault, but you came between us and I haven't quite figured out how to deal with that."

He held up his hands.

"That's cool," he said. "I get that. I mean, I wish I'd known you liked me sooner, because I think you're—" He met my eyes and then, another pink flush rising to his face, looked down at the floor. "What I mean is, I'm sorry. I just want to talk about all this stuff." He waved a hand vaguely around.

His eyes darted back up to mine as if to scope out whether it was safe. I forced a small smile onto my lips, then realized it didn't feel that forced.

"I'll bet this is a lot to take in," I said.

"I'm trying to roll with it."

I put a hand on the back of my chair and tapped it. "Let's go get food," I said. "At least I can answer your questions."

He brushed a lock of hair off his forehead with a nervous hand.

"That'd be really helpful."

I picked up my purse. I'd just arrived, but I knew Lorinda would let it slip. She only smiled at me as I left the building, though I could feel her curious gaze on us as we walked out of Wishes Fulfilled together and into the hall.

We stepped into the elevator together, and the doors slid shut. Instantly, as always happened in elevators, I was abruptly and acutely aware of his presence. He loomed in the corner, his Humdrum energy sparking and spiking every few seconds. His nerves felt about as frazzled as mine, but he hid it better.

We didn't look at each other or say anything during the whole ride down. When the elevator dinged and the doors slid open, he waited for me to get out first and then followed, his tennis shoes barely audible against the polished floor.

The theater we shared the building with had a lot of employees running around even during the day, and it wasn't unusual to run into a custodian or stagehand in the lobby in the afternoons. But the vaguely familiar woman standing in the lobby wasn't like the people I usually saw here. She stared at us, and over my glasses, a nebula of rose-pink swirls spun around her like a nervous tornado.

Her full lips and large black eyes made her seem larger than life and twice as beautiful. If I had to go on instinct alone, I'd say she had to be a Scheherazade Archetype, or someone from the Arabian Nights stories.

At the same time, she looked like the kind of person you might want for an older sister. Tufts of soft dark hair fell out of the loose braid slung over her shoulder. I kind of got the impression that, despite her stunning beauty and flawless posture, she just didn't care that much about how she looked.

I smiled, and her smile back was nothing more than a soft curve at the corner of her lips, though it managed to warm her whole face.

She had to be a client.

"We're upstairs," I said, and gestured toward the elevator.

I walked across the lobby toward the doors, trusting Lucas would follow.

My hand fell on the door.

"Wait," she said.

I turned. "Are you looking for Wishes Fulfilled?"

Usually, godparents came downstairs to meet their clients. Getting to our office was a challenge without help. I still wasn't sure how Lucas had managed it, seeing as how he wasn't supposed to even be able to see the glamoured top floor, let alone take an elevator up to it. But then, Lucas wasn't supposed to be involved in a lot of things.

The woman pursed her rosy lips and stared even more intently at me.

"I think I'm looking for you, actually," she said. "Are you Olivia Feye?"

EMMA SAVANT

The hair on my arms prickled. She seemed nice. But appearances weren't everything. Imogen had seemed nice, too. The Oracle had seemed sane. I knew better by now than to believe what was in front of me.

"I am," I said cautiously.

She glanced out the glass doors. I followed her gaze. The Oracle's Fountain sat there, quiet and ordinary in the morning sunlight. Humdrums walked past it, most of them not even glancing to where she lay in wait.

The woman came closer. Lucas' curiosity swelled beside me.

"I'm so glad to meet you," she said.

She held out a hand. I took it, and as I touched her warm skin, I caught a whiff of something that smelled like soil in spring.

"You know Evan Costner?" she said.

I pulled my hand back. This was not good news.

"My name is Isabelle Sheridan. I was Evan's fiancée," she said. "Until yesterday."

I lowered my glasses to look at her. Instantly, she settled into place in my memory. She'd been one of the models on Evan's website, and I'd seen a tiny version of her face in the comment she'd left.

Isabelle Sheridan.

The rose tornado rotated around her body.

Her face and energy seemed calm, not like she was about to curse me or sue me or do whatever scorned ex-lovers usually did in situations like this.

Still, I could barely stand under the weight of guilt.

"I'm so sorry," I said. "I tried to stop her."

"No," she said, holding up a hand. "I'm not here for that. You don't need to apologize."

"Thanks," I said. "Um, don't take this the wrong way, but you're Glimmering."

"I'm a hedge witch," she said. "Have been all my life."

"He didn't know?"

"No, of course not," she said. "But listen, I don't really want to talk about Evan. He's not why I'm here. I heard a rumor from a friend of mine. She's a water sprite."

Distaste rose up in me. The only water sprites I'd been hearing about lately were under the Oracle's thumb. I normally hated people who got all racist about magical subgroups, but today, prejudice rose up in me like thick, unwilling tar. I waited, and the woman stepped closer until she could speak in a low voice and still be heard.

"I work with roses," she said. "My sprite friend does, too. We were talking this morning and she said she heard you and I may be two of a kind." Her voice lowered until I had to strain to hear.

EMMA SAVANT

"I've been keeping an eye on this city for a while," she whispered.

That could mean anything. I frowned and waited. Lucas shifted beside me.

"Word among the sprites is that you had a little run-in with the Oracle," she said. "I heard all about it, and I liked what I heard."

"Yeah?" I said. I folded my arms. "How so?"

She leaned in. Her voice was soft as a rose petal against my ear.

"I think you're like me," she said. "I think you want to take the Oracle down."

I stepped back, stared at her, and waited for something to clue me in that this was a trick. If it was, though, Isabelle was a good enough actor to fool all my faerie senses. Sincerity flared off her like heat from a flame.

I glanced through the windows and at the Fountain, then back to her blazing black eyes. She was angry, I realized.

Almost as angry as me.

I leaned forward.

"How can I help?"

ABOUT THE AUTHOR

Emma Savant lives with her gorgeous husband and adorable cat in a small town in Oregon, where she spends way too much time watching *Star Trek* and eating nachos.

You can follow her online and be the first to hear about new Glimmers stories by visiting *www.EmmaSavant.com*.

www.ingramcontent.com/pod-product-compliance
Lightning Source LLC
Chambersburg PA
CBHW030644260626
47157CB00007B/2479